W9-CCP-109

Brownsburg Public Library

2 1201 91186 0531

LP M MACI
McInerny, Ralph M.
Irish coffee WITHDRAWN

IRISH COFFEE

Also by Ralph McInerny
in Large Print:

Irish Tenure
Emerald Aisle
Celt and Pepper
Grave Undertakings
Triple Pursuit
The Book of Kills
Lack of the Irish

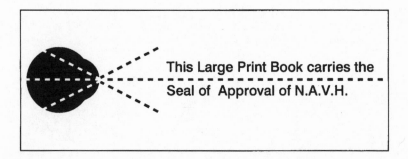

This Large Print Book carries the
Seal of Approval of N.A.V.H.

IRISH COFFEE

Ralph McInerny

Thorndike Press • Waterville, Maine

Brownsburg Public Library
450 South Jefferson Street
Brownsburg, Indiana 46112

Copyright © 2003 by Ralph McInerny.
A Mystery Set at the University of Notre Dame.

All rights reserved.

Published in 2004 by arrangement with
St. Martin's Press, LLC.

Thorndike Press® Large Print Basic.

The tree indicium is a trademark of Thorndike Press.

The text of this Large Print edition is unabridged.
Other aspects of the book may vary from the original edition.

Set in 16 pt. Plantin by Minnie B. Raven.

Printed in the United States on permanent paper.

Library of Congress Cataloging-in-Publication Data

McInerny, Ralph M.
    Irish coffee / Ralph McInerny.
      p. cm.
    ISBN 0-7862-6227-3 (lg. print : hc : alk. paper)
    1. Knight, Roger (Fictitious character) — Fiction.
    2. Knight, Philip (Fictitious character) — Fiction.
    3. Private investigators — Indiana — South Bend — Fiction.
    4. University of Notre Dame — Fiction.   5. South Bend
    (Ind.) — Fiction.   6. College teachers — Fiction.
    7. College sports — Fiction   8. Large type books.
    I. Title.
    PS3563.A31166I64 2004
      813´.54—dc22   2003068678

For Sally and Guy

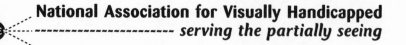

As the Founder/CEO of NAVH, the only national health agency solely devoted to those who, although not totally blind, have an eye disease which could lead to serious visual impairment, I am pleased to recognize Thorndike Press★ as one of the leading publishers in the large print field.

Founded in 1954 in San Francisco to prepare large print textbooks for partially seeing children, NAVH became the pioneer and standard setting agency in the preparation of large type.

Today, those publishers who meet our standards carry the prestigious "Seal of Approval" indicating high quality large print. We are delighted that Thorndike Press is one of the publishers whose titles meet these standards. We are also pleased to recognize the significant contribution Thorndike Press is making in this important and growing field.

Lorraine H. Marchi, L.H.D.
Founder/CEO
NAVH

★ Thorndike Press encompasses the following imprints: Thorndike, Wheeler, Walker and Large Print Press.

PART ONE

OUR MUTUAL FRIEND

I One golden October day, Roger and Philip Knight turned onto Notre Dame Avenue and as they neared Napoleon Boulevard Roger asked his brother to pull up in front of a venerable house of yellow brick. Roger regarded it with devotion and something like a nostalgic sigh escaped him.

"Who lives there?" Philip asked apprehensively. Did he fear that Roger had tired of their comfortable apartment in Notre Dame Village and was longing for them to have a home of their own again? Phil had shaken the dust of their house in Rye, New York, from his feet almost as willingly as he had left Manhattan some years earlier.

"It's the Lilac House."

"I don't see any."

"It's October. The University built this house for Maurice Francis Egan, one of the perks to lure him to Notre Dame."

"Ah."

"The name is not familiar?"

It was not familiar to Philip but it became so as they continued home. Stopped by the light at Angela Boulevard before they could turn east, their eyes were drawn

9

down the tree-lined avenue to the great pile of the Main Building and atop it, afire in the setting sun, the golden statue of Our Lady. Roger paused suitably and then continued his narration.

Maurice Francis Egan had been brought to Notre Dame by Father Sorin and named professor of literature, deserting the editorship of a New York newspaper to accept the offer. When the Main Building burned to the ground in 1879, Egan had edited a volume of poetry, the proceeds of the sales of which went to the rebuilding fund. How could Father Sorin fail to want to bind such a man more closely to Notre Dame? Hence the offer of a professorship and the construction of what Egan christened Lilac House, having planted lilac bushes all about the place. Roger's interest in Egan had taken its rise from Greg Whelan's remark that Roger's appointment to the Huneker Chair of Catholic Literature was reminiscent of Egan's Notre Dame connection.

"What do you have on him?" Roger had asked. Greg worked in the University archives.

"Lots."

And so he had. There were also some sixty books by Egan in the Hesburgh Library — poetry, novels, criticism, an appreciation of Leo XIII, an account of the Knights of Columbus in peace and war, and his delightful autobiography, *Recollections of a Happy Life*.

Roger had been a prodigy, recipient of a Princeton doctorate at the age of twenty-one, the year after he had converted to Catholicism. Age and his enormous weight, plus a paucity of positions in philosophy, led Roger, in a fit of romantic melancholy, to enlist in the navy. The recruiter, perhaps moved by the thought of what naval discipline might do for this unpromising physical specimen, had suitably altered Roger's application and into boot camp he had gone. There he had proved more of a problem than a challenge. He had passed the crucial swimming test by floating the length of the pool, mesmerized by the neon lighting above him. Assigned to the base library, he had wallowed and read for a year until a stern lieutenant commander had pronounced him unfit for his country's service. Discharged, he moved in with his brother, Philip, and, when the perils of life in Manhattan had proved too much, again moved with him to Rye where he had assisted Philip in his profession as private investigator. His monograph on Baron

11

Corvo appeared to rave reviews and modest sales and caught the eye of Father Carmody at Notre Dame in whose gift the newly endowed Huneker Chair of Catholic Studies effectively was. Roger's avoirdupois was not an impediment to professorial life; his learning and affability were weighty assets, and he had been offered and accepted the appointment. For three years, he had flourished in the classroom while Phil enjoyed access to the full spectrum of Notre Dame sports and continued his investigation business.

"Far more differences than similarities, Greg," Roger had said.

"At any rate I hope *you* won't be lured away by another university."

Maurice Francis Egan had left Notre Dame after less than a decade for a similar post at the nascent Catholic University of America. In Washington he had become a confidant of Theodore Roosevelt, and eventually spent a dozen years in Denmark as his country's representative. With that international career he sounded a good deal more like George Shuster than Roger Knight. But Roger was nonetheless grateful for having been put onto Maurice Francis Egan. Improbable as it seemed, it had been Maurice Francis Egan who occasioned Roger's friendship with Fred Neville.

After a brief stint in journalism, Fred, who had graduated in 1993, returned to Notre Dame as assistant to the sports information director and spent his days writing enigmatic press releases on the various athletic teams. He was tall and thin, round-shouldered and shy, and turned guiltily when Roger came upon him in the stacks on the eighth floor of the library, planted before a shelf containing the poetry and fiction of Maurice Francis Egan. Fred tried clumsily to return a book to the shelf, but it fell to the floor. He rose with it, face flushed, and tried to cover the title.

"*The Ghost in Hamlet*. You'll like it."

"You've read it?"

"I have made it a personal project to read everything Maurice Francis Egan ever wrote."

"*Confessions of a Book Lover*," said Fred.

"*The Wiles of Sexton Maginnis*," said Roger.

The litany continued, and then, "You're Roger Knight, aren't you? Professor Knight?"

"And you are?"

"Fred Neville."

Roger looked at the man. He was too old

13

to be a graduate student. Was he a new instructor in English?

"Good grief, no. I'm an amateur." He looked beyond Roger and said huskily, "I'm in the athletic department."

They went for coffee and that night Fred was their guest. Phil and Fred had the inexhaustible topic of Notre Dame athletics between them so a three-cornered friendship was formed. The brothers spelled one another, Roger talking books with Fred, Phil talking teams. The basketball season would soon be upon them and Roger listened to the two others discuss the prospects of the men's and women's teams in the upcoming season. Phil in turn listened patiently when Roger and Fred debated the merits of Maurice Francis Egan's poetry. Three happy bachelors. Sometimes four, when Greg joined them, the archivist's stammer disappearing when the conversation turned to Notre Dame lore. Often Roger and Greg, while a home game was in progress, visited in the Knights' apartment and if Phil returned with Fred, his duties done, the four consumed popcorn and talked into the wee hours. Phil was tolerant when the conversation drifted away from sports, waiting patiently until he could rescue Fred, as he thought it, from esoteric topics. Phil had tried to read an Egan novel but soon gave it up. The basketball season was off on a historic note and he could not believe the others could really be interested in stories written nearly a century before. After the women's team had clocked up their fifth straight victory he kept the conversation on a detailed analysis of the game. Fred seemed not to care what direction the discussion took.

The handouts Fred prepared for visiting newsmen betrayed some hints of his other interests. They were grammatical, with similes under a control not often found in press releases, and understated, Notre Dame athletics firmly lodged in the wider ambience of the university. From hockey to golf, from soccer to lacrosse, Fred's grasp of sports was formidable, a matter of wonderment to Phil. He could describe a football game played a quarter of a century ago as if he were giving a contemporary play-by-play account. But his passion was basketball. Only the most sensitive antenna could detect his preference for the men's team over the women's. In the privacy of the Knights' apartment, he could lament that the women too were turning the game into a contact sport.

"It should be a game of finesse," he said.

" 'Chess on the hardboards,' " Phil said. He was quoting one of Fred's press releases.

Players could be carried from the gridiron on stretchers, hockey players skate bloodied to the bench, but basketball should not be a danger to life and limb. He waxed poetic about Griselda Novak, the plucky little guard who was leading the Lady Irish to what promised to be a statistical dream of a season. Griselda came downcourt with effortless grace, surveying the defense before her, passed the ball with rifling accuracy or drifted through giants of the opposition to finger roll the ball into the hoop. Fred brushed aside suggestions that a pro career awaited the wily Griselda.

"She's on the honor roll. Basketball is a game for her. She could end up on the faculty."

"I have her in class," Roger said. "I had no idea she was an athlete."

Griselda was taking the course Roger was giving on writers who had been awarded the Laetare Medal and she had written an impressive paper on the woman who wrote under the pseudonym Christian Read. Griselda's honey-colored hair was worn in a ponytail on court and off and she did not walk with the rolling swagger of the woman athlete. She had even played a small role in a campus production in Washington Hall and an unctuous account went out from the sports publicity department, authored by Fred.

"She has stolen your heart away," Roger teased.

Fred blushed. There was a moment of silence. In that celibate gathering, the attraction of female beauty was seldom alluded to. That Fred might be smitten by Griselda or some woman of more appropriate age seemed briefly possible. But the moment passed and the blood drained from Fred's face. The teasing suggestion that the eloquent member of the sports information office might be a Lothario was not pursued.

2   Griselda Novak was that rarity among Notre Dame undergraduates, a native of South Bend. Her parents had succumbed to the dissolution of the ethnic west side of the city and migrated north to the sprawling suburb of Granger, which was why Griselda had attended Penn High School rather than St. Joseph's like her parents. The athletic program at Penn rivaled that of many colleges and Griselda had distinguished herself in both soccer and basketball, had been the subject of two laudatory profiles by the normally acerbic Hough of the *South Bend Tribune*, a paper Jim Novak, Griselda's father, subscribed to only for the sake of the obituaries and the sports page. Its editorials and featured op-ed columnists turned this habitually laconic lawyer into a muttering, sputtering, red-faced critic. Among his few confessable faults was to accuse his wife of sounding like Molly Ivens. But it was with Griselda rather than his wife that he discussed the news of the day. Griselda wrote for the school paper in a way that warmed her father's heart and she was an excellent student all around. It never occurred to the

Novaks that her athletic accomplishments were anything more than grace notes to her schooling. Other parents with less gifted sons or daughters brooded over their children's future in sports and dreamed the dreams of avarice. A tennis player might be groomed for the pros, a gifted golfer be nurtured for future professional play. It was not unheard of that ambitious parents sought the advice of sports agents to advance the careers of their children. Not the Novaks. Griselda was a Merit Scholar and had been admitted to Notre Dame as a student. When Muffin McGraw saw Griselda in the bookstore tournament the coach urged Griselda to become a walk-on member of the women's basketball team where she soon outshone those who had been lured to South Bend with athletic scholarships. She loved the game but eschewed the role of jock. It was a fateful day when she signed up for Roger Knight's seminar devoted to Chesterton and Belloc. She had taken a course from him every semester since. A fissure appeared in her soul and had been widening ever since.

"Have you read everything that was ever written?" she asked Roger one afternoon. She had taken the wheel of the golf cart in which Roger got around the campus and at his direction driven to Grace where they sat at an outdoor table over coffee.

Roger laughed. "Hardly. But there are certain authors I read again and again."

"I want to be like you."

"Fat?"

"You should work out, you know."

"Lose weight?"

"You could."

"Oh, I have. But like the devil in Scripture who was driven out of a man but returned with seven others, the last state of that man was worse than the first."

Griselda thought about it. "I think you're right. God wants you fat."

"You make it sound meritorious."

Roger's enormous weight and childlike manner brought out the mother in female undergraduates. Griselda had seen this in others and knew her own case to be different. She regretted talking to him about exercise. He was everything a professor ought to be. Her teammates dreamed of playing professional ball, her classmates contemplated various worldly futures, but sitting in Roger Knight's class had made Griselda realize that the campus was goal enough for her.

"I want to go on in English and then come back here on the faculty."

He did not dismiss this possibility. He began to talk to her about graduate programs. They went on to discuss Christian Read, a woman novelist who had been one of the recipients of the Laetare Medal.

"Father Hudson was the editor of *Ave Maria* magazine, a pet project of Father Sorin's. It no longer exists but in its day it was one of the most influential Catholic magazines. When Christian Read — the pen name of Frances Tiernan — was given the medal, Father Hudson and Father Zahm traveled to Alabama to confer it on her at Belmont Abbey."

One of the fascinating things about Roger Knight was his knowledge of the history of Notre Dame. Everyone knew about Notre Dame athletics but Professor Knight talked of the faculty giants of the nineteenth-century and early twentieth-century Notre Dame as if they were colleagues. It was with growing reluctance that Griselda went off to the Joyce Center for practice. Once on the court, however, she was absorbed in the game. The team had started off the season with a bang and already there was talk of another banner being hung from the rafters in recognition of postseason accomplishment. But after practice, walking through the twilit campus to her room, Griselda felt that she was returning to her real reason for being at Notre Dame. Back at her books, she regretted the time she had to put in practicing. One practiced in order to play and she loved to play, particularly at home when the student section was crammed and all the other seats filled with twelve thousand fans, but after all, basketball is only a game. She was wise enough not to speak such heresy to the coaches or her teammates. Though, Fred Neville might understand. After all, he was a friend of Roger Knight's.

3   In his office in the Joyce Athletic and Convocation Center Fred Neville sat with his hands poised over the keyboard of his computer like a pianist waiting out the strings before rejoining the concerto. On the screen before him short uneven lines awaited completion. Fred's lips moved contemplatively as he ran through words rhyming with *dust*. The assistant sports information director was dropping into poetry. The lines on the monitor represented one complete stanza and the partial one on which he had become stuck. A face appeared around the open doorway, Pryzwara, one of the assistant basketball coaches.

"Spell my name right," Pryzwara said and advanced grinning into the office. Fred hastily changed screens on his computer.

"I can spell it but no one can pronounce it."

Pryzwara pronounced his name several times. It sounded like a Bronx cheer.

"Coming with us to Dayton, Fred?"

"Not my turn."

"Just prepare a release on a victory."

23

Pryzwara sat. Fred had already switched gears. For ten minutes he discussed the strengths and weaknesses of the team the Irish would face in Dayton.

"Tell me about Digger and UCLA."

Fred told him. Both he and Pryzwara had been boys when under Digger Phelps the Notre Dame basketball team had won an historic victory over the legendary John Wooden's previously unbeaten UCLA team, a victory that ranked with Rockne's win over Army, another contest Fred could recount as if he had been an eyewitness. Pryzwara sat rapt through the recital.

"Wooden was a high school coach in South Bend before he went on to college coaching."

"You're a walking archive, Fred." Pryzwara rose, clapped him on the back and headed for the door. "Want the door left open?"

"Better close it."

The door closed. Fred let a minute go by and then brought up the broken lines of his poem and stared at them. Inspiration had fled. He opened a drawer of his desk and looked at a photograph there without taking it out. He sighed and turned again to his monitor.

Shakespeare, thou shouldst be living
  at this hour
For only you could catch in words her face
Her eyes, her lips, her look as of a flower
Open to the sun, abloom with grace.

But golden lasses must alas to dust
Return, become with autumn gray,
And she . . .

Here the muse had deserted him and Pryzwara's visit had filled his mind again with the lore that was his stock-in-trade. He stored the unfinished poem in the file he had labeled *Egan,* stole another look at the photograph in his drawer and was suddenly overwhelmed by the futility of his mad desire to match the literary output of Maurice Francis Egan.

"Assistant sports information director," he said aloud and there was derision in his voice.

As an undergraduate his only publications had appeared in the back pages of *The Observer,* in sports, the pieces that along with those he had written as a journalist in Toledo had been the basis of his return to campus and the sports information office. His position should have made him proud — he knew a dozen men

BROWNSBURG PUBLIC LIBRARY

who would kill to take his place — but he sat in his office and repined. His friendship with the Knight brothers, Phil and Roger, summed up his dilemma. He could regale Phil with items from the history of Notre Dame athletics but it was when he talked with Roger that his heart was full. In the Knight apartment he could reveal his first love and speak with Roger of literature, of Maurice Francis Egan and other literary heroes. But not even to Roger had he confessed that he aspired to be something more than a consumer of the works of others. Not even to Roger could he admit the contents of the file called *Egan*.

There was a knock on the door.

It was Muffin McGraw, coach of the Lady Irish, short-skirted, high-heeled, a look of tragic concern on her little face.

"We've got a problem." She sat and looked at Fred with wide eyes. "Griselda."

"Was she injured in practice?"

"She said she might leave the team."

"Leave the team!" Fred's expression now matched the coach's. A team without Griselda Novak was an internal combustion engine without a distributor. He made a mental note of the simile, praying he would never have to use it.

"Talk to her, Fred."

"Me?"

"She raves about you. You could influence her. You've got to talk sense to her."

"I will. What's the problem?"

"She wants to become a professor. She feels she is wasting valuable time playing basketball." McGraw whispered these words as a believer might repeat the blasphemy of an infidel.

"Ah."

"Will you talk to her?"

"Of course I'll talk to her. She can't quit the team. She is the very definition of the student athlete. She can do both."

"Bless you, Fred. Tell her that. Are you going to Dayton with the men?"

"No."

"Good. Talk to her tonight."

He took Griselda to dinner at Parisi's from which an unimpeded view of the illuminated golden dome was visible.

"Just us?"

"I couldn't get hold of Roger." This implied that he had tried, which was a lie. But he had to be alone with Griselda. It was clear to Fred that Roger Knight was the origin of her problem.

"His class is wonderful."

"Tell me about it."

A tactical mistake. Fred was drawn by her admiration for their mutual friend and soon they were discussing Roger's account of nineteenth-century female Catholic novelists.

"He recognizes their limitations of course. But he emphasizes their good points. That's how he differs from the others. He isn't interested in scoring easy points."

"Scoring points is never easy."

"You should sit in on some of my classes."

"Muffin dropped in on me today."

A toss of her ponytail. "Hence this unusual invitation."

"She thinks you are considering giving up basketball."

"Look, I can talk to you. You know Roger. What would you rather be, a pro athlete who burns out in a couple of years never more to be seen, or someone like him?"

She had stated his own dilemma and he felt the falsity of his position. How could he argue against a sentiment that was his own. "Not a choice I have to make."

"But what if it's mine?"

"You want to be a female version of Roger Knight."

"Even a pale copy would do. He can go on doing what he is doing forever. Today in class he talked about Maurice Francis Egan. Do you know him?"

"Yes."

"I'd never even heard the name before. That's why his class is exciting. Not only is it taught at Notre Dame, it *is* Notre Dame. Why do people think this place begins and ends with Knute Rockne?"

"No one thinks that."

"Meaning you don't. What do the coaches and players know of the real Notre Dame?"

The point of this dinner was to make the case for Griselda's continuing to play basketball. But Fred found that he was more sympathetic to Griselda's doubts about a life in sports, meaning as she had said a few years in the pros and then what? Color commentary on a cable network, waxing enthusiastic about each new crop of players.

" 'A veritable snowstorm of virginity.' "

"What?"

"Christopher Fry."

"Did he teach here?"

"No."

"Fred, I know you understand what I'm saying. How long have you known Roger Knight?"

"I think you should talk to him about this."

"So do I. But Muffin asked me to talk to you first."

She'd had half a glass of wine and he finished the bottle. The dinner was on his expense account. He was light-headed when they went out to his car.

"Look," she said, pointing at the golden dome.

"The dome that Sorin built."

"Do you want me to drive?"

"I'm okay."

She punched his arm. "I can see why Roger likes you so much."

That was the one remark of the evening that stayed with him. For now, Griselda could play basketball and be a student and then choose what future she would.

4 Marjorie Shuster's husband had taught in the government department during the days when Gerhardt Niemeir and Stephen Kertecz had set the tone of the department. It was political philosophy then, not a lesser branch of the social sciences riddled with statistics and supposedly objective analyses. Vision had already begun to dim when Nathaniel Shuster died, leaving Marjorie to raise Mary. There had never been any question of leaving Notre Dame and Marjorie stayed on in their home in Harter Heights. She had gone to work in the library and eventually, after graduating, Mary got a job in admissions. They might have been carrying on a family tradition. But Marjorie would not have been a mother if she did not say novena after novena, praying that Mary would find the right man, have a family, gild Marjorie's later years with grandchildren. But Mary was nearing thirty and there was no man in prospect and Marjorie was becoming desperate. She herself had married at twenty-one. A sign of her desperation was that, when Roger Knight arrived on campus, she began to cultivate him as a potential son-

in-law. Marjorie could hardly question her daughter's failure to see in the enormous Huneker professor a possible mate. For all that, they became fast friends. And there was Philip.

"I'm surprised you're not married," Marjorie said to Phil in that voice women adopt when the good of the race is at issue.

"You wouldn't be if you knew what I come across in my line of work."

"I don't understand."

"A private investigator could make a fortune dealing only with wives who want to get rid of their husbands or husbands who want to get rid of their wives. I've seen too much of it."

"Is that what you do for a living?"

"I'm in semiretirement since Roger and I moved here."

"So you made your fortune from disgruntled spouses."

"Oh, I never handled divorces, not after one or two of them. In fact, I explicitly ruled them out."

"And your views haven't mellowed." Marjorie had recovered her matchmaking voice.

"Even if they had, it's a little late for that sort of thing."

"Oh bosh." She looked him over with the calculating eye of a carnival guesser. He was lean whereas Roger was . . . well, there was a lot to Roger. Phil's blond hair was graying in a way women paid large sums to match. And he was tall. Marjorie liked a tall man, a preference she never referred to her late husband, the five-seven Professor Nathaniel Shuster. "If you're fifty I'll eat your hat."

Phil fetched a Notre Dame cap and handed it to her. "Or would you like it cooked?"

"You're not yet fifty?"

"I'll get you another hat."

But there was a lot to say for a mature man who had seen a lot of the world. A woman who put her mind to it could alter his cynical notion of marriage. But was Mary the woman? An overture of the most oblique kind elicited trilling laughter from her daughter. "Philip Knight! That old bachelor."

"Most men are bachelors before they get married."

"I'd rather marry Roger."

"Then do it, for heaven's sake."

"Oh Mother."

"You know how old we are going to be on our next birthday."

Marjorie wished Mary would not laugh in that derisive way.

"Mother, when I fall in love I'll keep it a secret until the wedding day."

"*When* you fall in love?"

"*If* I fall in love."

So it was back to the novenas. Was the response to her prayers that the Knight brothers became their good friends despite her efforts on Mary's behalf? From time to time Roger would reciprocate for dinners at the Shusters by putting on one of his virtuoso performances in the kitchen. How he managed it when he prepared quantities sufficient for a regiment she never knew, but his *risotto con funghi e piselli* was fluffy and perfectly seasoned, his quiche lorraine exquisite. But he took as much pride in his popcorn as anything else. They had been invited over to watch Notre Dame play Dayton on television, and Gregory Whelan was there as well. A mute rather than a mate, Marjorie had cruelly decided long ago, though when Mary and Roger talked away about God knows what while Marjorie and Phil followed the game, the unfamiliar and fluent voice of the archivist was heard. But the excitement of the game soon drove such thoughts from Marjorie's head. It was still halftime when Fred

Neville showed up with Griselda Novak in tow.

All the men sprang to their feet as the star athlete came in. Mary on the other hand turned her back on the huddle that formed around Griselda and joined her mother before the television set.

"Who is he?"

"Someone with Griselda, obviously."

"Griselda!" She was but a girl.

"They've been out to dinner."

"Really."

Another little balloon of hope floated away. If only Mary would show a little interest something might happen but she had visibly snubbed the newcomer. Phil came back and dropped into his chair just as the second half was about to begin.

"Who's the man?" asked Marjorie.

"Man? That's Fred Neville. I'll introduce him during a commercial."

But Fred Neville had taken Roger aside and Griselda wandered in and sat on the floor.

"Who's winning?" she asked.

Mary ignored her; Phil was absorbed in the game. Marjorie said, "I think we are."

Maybe she shouldn't have said that. In a game anything can happen. And Marjorie felt that any project she backed was doomed. But Mary, bless her heart, was now sitting on the arm of Phillip's chair and turning on the charm. However weary from past jumps, hope springs eternal. What a wonderful couple they would make, Mary and Philip Knight.

5 Roger had been thoroughly briefed by Fred Neville on Griselda's threat to leave the team.

"She is a real student, and thank God for it, but the thing about Notre Dame is that athletes are students. Well, most of them. Of course I understand that Griselda should be excited about the world you've opened up to her."

"What am I to say to her?"

"That she can do both. She will be pressured to turn pro after she graduates but she can deal with that when the time comes. Roger, it would be a disaster if she left the team."

"I should think you would be a persuasive argument for doing both, Fred. You are far more interesting to talk with than some of my strictly academic colleagues."

Fred tried not to beam but he was clearly delighted by such praise. And Roger meant it. Any surprise he had felt that the assistant sports information director was a learned devotee of literature had long since passed. Phil might be surprised at Fred's dual competency but

Roger had learned that Fred's heart was in the authors they discussed. A mention of the dictionary Baron Corvo described at the beginning of *Hadrian VII* had fascinated Fred and he had drawn on his undergraduate minor in classics to a spoofing version of his own.

"The point is to create a bogus Latin vocabulary. What do you suppose *sububi* means?"

"Tell me."

"Underwear. *Sub* and *ubi*. 'Overhead' is *supercaput.*"

Roger suggested a mad meaning for *propter quid*. "An athlete's chaw."

Pretty bad, but that was the point. "Do you know Ambrose Bierce's *Devil's Dictionary?*"

He was trying to deflect Fred from the reason for his visit. Roger had no stomach for advising Griselda in so important a matter but Fred enlisted Phil, who was shocked by the possibility that Griselda might quit the basketball team.

"You've got to talk sense to her, Roger."

But it was with foreboding that Roger asked Griselda to wait for him after class. Other students hung on and Roger welcomed this, half-hoping that Griselda would have to leave. But she remained.

They went again to the eatery in Grace.

It was an Indian summer day. The trees were gold and brown, sun shone, a banner hanging from the windows of Zahm Hall flapped in the slight breeze. *God Made Notre Dame #1.* An acceptable assertion in Mariology at least.

"Does the phrase *men sana in corpore sano* mean anything to you?"

"I never took Spanish. Not yet," she added.

He did not correct her. "You have caused despair in the athletic department."

"So Fred talked to you."

"If you'd rather not . . ."

"Of course I want to talk to you. Fred tried to but he's in love and isn't thinking straight."

"Griselda, he took you to dinner in the line of duty."

She stared at him a moment before laughing merrily. "Not with me!"

Roger was confused. He had no idea what Griselda had meant. So far as he knew, Fred was as confirmed a bachelor as himself and Phil.

"You know who I mean," Griselda said.

Roger found that he was unwilling to discuss this surprising suggestion. Phil had told Roger of Marjorie's attempt at matchmaking. Had she succeeded with Fred? It would have seemed a breach of friendship to talk about it with Griselda.

"Let's get back to you."

He formulated for her the argument Fred had sketched, one Roger truly believed in. Nature had put enmity between himself and sports and he had never developed a fan's interests, but he almost envied Phil's and Fred's enthusiasm for sports.

"When I was in the navy I had to pass a swimming test."

"You were in the navy?"

"Only briefly."

"But that's wonderful. Tell me about it."

His naval career, however thwarted, provided a surprising wedge. Roger could see that Griselda imagined him fit and trim in bell-bottoms, his hat cocked jauntily on his head. He could read in her expression an imagined prowess in himself.

"I spent most of my enlistment in the base library reading."

"Even then you did both."

"Exactly." Well, perhaps inexactly. No need to tell her of his ignominious exit from the navy. At the time he had felt a twinge of disappointment. It was rather a good library of its kind.

"And you can do both. Think of how well you are doing in my class."

"Your class is unique." She thought for a moment. "There aren't a lot of other classes I would want to take if I had more time. I'd like to major in Roger Knight."

"You have to know what professors to take. I could advise you. But there is really no reason for you to let down the basketball team. Sports are part of Notre Dame. You are very fortunate that you can represent the university."

"I do like to play."

"Because you do it well. I would never forgive myself if your interest in my class led to your deserting the team."

"What are you teaching next semester?"

"Dante and Ezra Pound."

"Wow."

The conversation had taken a happy turn. He told her about T. S. Eliot's lectures on the metaphysical poets, of Santayana's little book *Three Philosophical Poets*. He told her of Pound's editing of *The Waste Land* and the implied comparison represented by his own cantos. Griselda hunched over the table, fascinated.

"I want to be like you," she said. "I told you that before and I meant it."

"When is basketball season over?"

41

"I'll have most of next semester to my-self."

"So there you are."

She nodded. "If you could pass swimming, I can play basketball."

And so the crisis passed and Griselda continued to play, becoming even more impressive than before, executing the plays, the commander on the floor. Muffin McGraw was grateful.

"Some professors might have encouraged her to quit."

"Oh, I doubt that."

"It is a demanding schedule, but Griselda handles basketball and her classes better than anyone I've known. She doesn't even have a tutor."

Fred just shook his hand wordlessly, his expression telling the gratitude he felt. Roger did not mention that his floating the length of the pool was his greatest achievement as a naval swimmer. Griselda had made more of that feat than it deserved but it seemed an innocent deception.

"That kid will be a pro," Phil said, watching Griselda lead the Lady Irish to victory over the fabled University of Connecticut's women's basketball team. They were called UConn, which suggested

Alaska, but Griselda put the freeze on them.

"We'll see."

And then tragedy struck.

In the second week of November, Fred did not appear at his desk in the Joyce Center. On the second day, when there was no response to messages left on his telephone, Roger went to check. He persuaded the caretaker of the building to let him into the apartment, a flashing display of his private detective's license the open sesame. Fred Neville lay dead in his bed.

6 The wake for Fred Neville was held in Hickey's Funeral Home on Cleveland Road and all Notre Dame teams were heavily represented by coaches and players, something Phil took great pride in.

"What a turnout, Roger."

Fred's parents were equally impressed. Mr. and Mrs. Neville had flown in from their retirement home in Phoenix, stunned by the news. At their age, it was their own death that had seemed proximate, and now their only son was dead at the height of his powers.

"He e-mailed us everything he wrote," Mr. Neville said. Mrs. Neville, a little woman with large almond eyes, nodded.

"Everything."

"He will be sorely missed," Roger assured them. It was a phrase the Nevilles would hear again and again during the taxing hours of the wake. Father Molloy came to lead the rosary, one of several dozen members of the Holy Cross community who came to pay their respects. Monk Molloy had been a basketball player in his day and not even the presidency of Notre

Dame could compete with that fact in his personal estimation. He was still a familiar figure on the outdoor courts for pickup games and never missed a home game when he was in town, sitting in taciturn appraisal as priests around him leapt up and cheered at any provocation. But Monk sat with folded arms in more contemplative appreciation of the feats of the team.

Roger had seen Marjorie Shuster enter the viewing room and sign the book and he crossed the room to join her. She turned her large sad eyes on him.

"Have you seen Mary?"

"Isn't she with you?"

"She came early. She said she wanted to be here for the whole four hours." There was that in Marjorie's tone that filled Roger with apprehension. "Look, she's on the prie-dieu."

And there indeed she was, clad all in black with a black mantilla on her head as she stared in desolation at the body of Fred Neville. She might have been a widow.

That, as it turned out, was the explanation of Marjorie's tone. She leaned toward Roger and whispered, "She says they were engaged."

"Engaged."

"Can you believe it?"

The thought disturbed Roger's prayers when he himself lowered his enormous body onto the prie-dieu before the open casket and stared at the body of his friend. Mary was now seated prominently in the second seat in the front row and when Father Molloy sat beside her before beginning the rosary she wept silently. The puzzled Nevilles sat in the same row. Mary embraced Mrs. Neville and lifted her face for Mr. Neville's kiss. His dry lips pressed against her mantilla. They were clearly as surprised as Marjorie. Few in the room failed to notice Mary's mourning apparel and her look of unutterable grief. Roger and Phil took Marjorie home for a fortifying drink.

"Just a little Jameson's," she said. "No, make it a lot."

"Ice?"

"Water. Just a little."

And then she told her story. Mary had been hysterical when she heard the news, already something of a surprise, and then she had told her mother she was engaged to marry Fred.

"She claims they had been engaged for months."

"Claims?"

"I know nothing about it."

"Do daughters always tell such secrets to their mothers?"

"They do when they live as close as we do. We have no secrets."

"The night she was here and Fred came in she acted as if she didn't know him."

"I said the same thing. Apparently, she was peeved because he came in with Griselda Novak!"

The ways of women were a mystery to the Knight brothers. "I wonder if Fred knew."

But Roger remembered Griselda's remark about Fred being in love. Had she meant Mary Shuster? He went into his study and made a call.

"Isn't it awful?" Griselda said. "I saw you at the wake but didn't get a chance to talk to you."

"You remember Mary Shuster, the woman who was here the night . . ."

"She's his girl. Or she was. I often caught them smooching in his office. She visited him there a lot."

This would be confirmed by others in the Joyce Center. Marjorie and the Knights seemed the only ones who hadn't known of Fred and Mary. When his desk was opened some days later, her photograph was found.

Marjorie said, "Why would she keep it a secret? The reason she gave made no sense."

"What was that?"

Marjorie hesitated. "She said I nagged her so much about being single she didn't want me whooping it up if she told me."

"Of course she would have told you eventually."

"Look at what *eventually* turned out to mean. The girl is making a spectacle of herself."

"You can't blame her for mourning Fred."

"All in black? She never brought him home, not once, to introduce him to her mother. If I knew nothing about it, who did? And there she was, acting like a widow. How can you be a widow if you never married?"

"*Our Mutual Friend*," Roger murmured.

The reference sailed past Marjorie. "Oh, I know, I know. It isn't that I didn't like the man, what I knew of him, God rest his soul. She did this out of spite."

"Now, Marjorie."

"Well, what am I to think? Keeping something like this from her own mother. If it's even true. Do you have any more of this, Phil?"

"A little."

48

"That's all I want."

Marjorie seemed intent on having an Irish wake for Fred Neville, the son-in-law that might have been.

"I suppose it's a blessing, God forgive me. What did he die of?"

Phil said, "He died in his sleep."

Phil drove Marjorie home and Roger asked to be taken along. "Drop me at Hickey's, Phil."

"You're going back there? Talk to Mary, please."

Thus it was that Roger was at the funeral home when Naomi McTear appeared.

She was a slender girl with thick red hair worn to her shoulders, familiar as the breathless reporter from the sidelines at televised football games, the one that buttonholed a coach as he was heading for the locker room at halftime. Her dress was modish, festive rather than mourning. She stood in the open door of the viewing room and looked around at the depleted group. Then she saw the Nevilles and walked rapidly to them as if she were going to conduct an interview. She gathered Mrs. Neville into her arms, her left hand splayed on the back of the smaller woman. She was wearing the biggest diamond Roger had ever seen.

"Phyllis," she sobbed.

"Naomi."

Then she turned to Mr. Neville. "Oh, Arthur, Arthur." It was he who embraced her and she looked up at him, all tears. Then she glanced at the casket and shuddered. She broke free and went to the casket where she stood, hands at her hips, staring at the body. Not ten feet away, Mary Shuster studied the new arrival. She had seen the greeting she received from the Nevilles — who hadn't? Someone approached the Nevilles and then the word went around.

"She's Fred's fiancée. Naomi McTear."

PART TWO

PORTRAIT OF
A LADY

I The bells of Sacred Heart basilica tolled mournfully on the Friday, prelude to the funeral Mass for Fred Neville. Snow had begun to fall during the night, falling on the living and the dead, and students tramping through it to dining hall or early class heard without hearing the tolling bells. Few of them would have heard of Fred Neville, let alone his death. A decade ago he had been one of them, indifferent to the liturgies that went on in the campus church, weddings, funerals, baptisms. The hall chapels were the site of such devotions as students engage in. Sacred Heart was for special occasions. Students could be pardoned if they did not regard Fred Neville's funeral as a special occasion.

There are four seasons at Notre Dame, of course, but students know only three of them and fall and winter are the only ones whose beginning and end they observe on campus. Despite the excitement of football in the fall, winter is the season most will remember in future years, the campus walks winding between piles of shoveled snow, the leafless trees exposed in their spectral beauty, mere sketches of what they have been and will be again. In winter the world awaits its resurrection, spring is the Easter season when ducks and geese and swans move about on the melted lakes, and for seniors commencement looms. It is an academic conceit that the end of their time at Notre Dame should be called a beginning, but so in a way it is, for then they will join the great silent majority, the quick and the dead, that have walked this campus and, however little remembered, take indelible memories of it with them when they go. So it had been with Fred Neville with the difference that he had returned to find himself an almost-stranger in a place that had marked him for life. And now he was definitively gone.

Last night, when he had returned to the funeral home a second time and witnessed the arrival of Naomi McTear, Roger had received disturbing news. A hand was laid on his arm and he turned to face Lieut. Jimmy Stewart of the South Bend police.

"Is your brother with you?"

"He will be picking me up."

"Good. Let's go in here."

Jimmy Stewart led Roger down the hall to an empty room much like the one in which the body of Fred Neville lay.

"We may have a problem, Roger."

"Hence your presence?"

He nodded. "Apparently it wasn't an accidental death."

There had been an autopsy, just routine because Fred had been dead some days before his body was discovered and, while the usual tests were being run, the body had been turned over to the undertaker.

"No problem there, though we may postpone burial."

"You don't mean the funeral won't take place."

"That can go on. Why not? But the body will be brought downtown to the morgue."

"Good Lord. His parents have come, all kinds of people will expect to accompany the body to Cedar Grove Cemetery."

This cemetery was on campus, on Notre Dame Avenue just south of the bookstore, not to be confused with the community cemetery where members of the Congregation of Holy Cross were laid to rest in their own private Arlington under identical crosses, row on row. That was located off the road that led from the Grotto to St. Mary's College across the highway.

Phil came half an hour later, having got Marjorie safely to her door and through it.

"She chattered all the way home," Phil

said. And then he noticed Jimmy Stewart. "What's up?"

Jimmy Stewart took Phil away and put him in the picture. Roger returned to the viewing room and walked slowly up to the casket and stared at Fred with far different emotions than he had prayed for him earlier. He had been poisoned. When the report was given to him, Jimmy Stewart had gone to Fred's apartment, which was untouched although of course it had not yet been declared a crime scene. The Nevilles had postponed visiting their son's apartment until after the funeral, before they planned to return to Phoenix. There was no one else to clean up the place. Jimmy Stewart had taken the coffee mug from the table beside the bed downtown to the lab. In it were traces of the poison that had sent Fred into the next world. A dreadful thought had occurred to Roger. Had Fred administered the poison to himself?

"There wasn't a note?" Roger asked.

"I didn't really look. The apartment is sealed now of course and we will be going over it thoroughly."

Nothing Roger knew of Fred suggested that he would kill himself but the events of the evening had made Roger wonder how well he knew his friend. He had been revealed to have a fiancée, whom he had never mentioned, Mary Shuster had appointed herself principal mourner, and there were indications that there had indeed been something between her and Fred. How little we know others, even those to whom we are close. He and Fred had spent so many happy hours talking, and he had sensed that Fred could be open with him about his non-athletic interests; there was an implicit confidentiality clause in all their conversations. It seemed impossible that Fred would not at least have hinted at his feelings, whatever they had been, for Mary. Griselda had certainly no doubt what they were; she was sure Fred and Mary had been in love.

But Roger thought of the evening when Fred had come to the apartment after dining with Griselda, to enlist Roger in the campaign to prevent her from leaving the basketball team, and Mary and her mother were there. There was little indication the two had even known one another. Indeed, Mary had all but snubbed Fred. Jealousy? The vast mystery of every human person struck Roger forcibly, as it often had before. What we say and do reveals who we are, up to a point, but one is a mystery to himself so how can we expect to penetrate the soul of another? The investigation that was about to begin would uncover many facts hitherto unknown — investigations always did — but they would only deepen the mystery, not dissolve it.

When he and Phil returned to their apartment, they sat up late discussing this surprising turn of events.

"He give you any clue he might do this, Roger?"

"Does Jimmy Stewart think it was suicide?"

"Why would anyone else kill him?"

"Why would he kill himself, Phil?"

Phil assumed his professional persona. "Whether or not he did has to be established before we ask why."

It was nearly eleven when Father Carmody showed up unannounced. They had acknowledged one another at the funeral home but that was all. Now it was clear that Father Carmody had learned how Fred had died.

"You have to be our liaison with the police, Phil. We can't have a scandal."

"Jimmy Stewart is the investigating officer."

"Is that good?"

"Very good."

Father Carmody looked relieved. The

58

old priest was the unofficial custodian of the university's reputation, a man whose whole life had been lived here. He had come to Notre Dame as a teenager, when there was a preparatory seminary on campus, and lived his whole life at the university. So many things that had been personal experiences of Father Carmody were matters of history to others. He had been instrumental in Roger's being appointed the Huneker Professor of Catholic Studies, making him a free variable on campus, able to cross-list the courses he chose to give in several departments.

"You two knew him, didn't you?"

"Yes."

"His poor parents," the priest said. "I had just a few words with them. Wonderful people. They were bearing up well under the blow of his death, but what will their reaction to this news be?"

Fred's death had been blow enough, but now the manner of his going would provide a testing time for his parents and doubtless for the two women he seemed to be connected with. And of course for his friends. Roger was glad that Phil would have a quasi-official role in the investigation.

So it was with mixed emotions indeed

that Roger and Phil had gotten out of their car and walked slowly to the basilica with the bells tolling overhead.

2   A funeral Mass is not what it was. Not so long ago, the priest was vested in black, yellow rather than white candles stood on the altar, the sermon was devoted to generic remarks about the fragility of life and the certainty of mortality. And the lugubrious Dies Irae was sung. The liturgy was solemn and somber, all in Latin and conducted in the guarded hope that the deceased had made it into purgatory at best where the sins of a lifetime must be washed away. The chaste tones of Gregorian chant rode their measured scale. Dante's great poem depicted this halfway house to heaven as a seven-story mountain, up which the soul must painfully climb as it was purged of the effects of the capital sins. The stakes of life were put earnestly before those still living, and for the departed was implored an eventual entrance into paradise.

It is thus no longer. The tendency is to speak of the deceased as even now enjoying the beatific vision, swept up from a sinful life immediately into the presence of God. The homily is often an untroubled celebration of the life that has ended, given in the sunny conviction that the congregation was marking the passing of a saint. There is little somber about it, however grief-stricken the family might be. But grief is masked with smiles. A kind of jolly universalism is in the air, as if everyone must be destined for eternal bliss, with no suggestion that there could be any delay in entering into it. Seldom are lessons drawn for those who fill the pews.

Fred Neville's funeral struck a middle note between these two extremes. There was no eulogy of the deceased during the liturgy. Naomi McTear was prominent in the first pew beside the Nevilles, her claim upon the departed thus dramatically endorsed. But the first reading called this into question. Mary Shuster, clad all in black, her mantilla shading her eyes, appeared in the pulpit and read in clear and tragic tones the words of the epistle. Her tone, her manner, her dress, proclaimed her to be chief among the mourners. The church was hushed when she first appeared, the silence deepened as she read and when she concluded with "The Word of the Lord," she might have been enlisting the almighty in her claim to be the bereft beloved of Fred Neville. She slowly lifted her bowed head and for half a minute stared out at the congregation in silence.

Then she turned to descend and was lost from view. As if in relief, there was stirring in the pews and throats were cleared.

Jimmy Stewart was in the choir loft where Philip Knight joined him. Father Carmody's homily would have fitted well into the old liturgy, that into which he had been ordained and whose passing he lamented. He mentioned Fred by name, he noted the presence of the grieving parents, he reminded the congregation that though weep they must they should not weep as those without hope. And he urged prayers for the departed, that his soul might rest in peace. For the living he prayed for the grace of a happy death. Fred was neither canonized nor condemned, but the great mystery of death and our universal need for mercy was made clear to all. Roger Knight was comforted but not surprised that Father Carmody had found just the right words.

In the sanctuary were a dozen priests of the Congregation of Holy Cross; Father Molloy was the celebrant. The turnout was a show of respect for the deceased and a boost for the athletic department. Coaches, their spouses, and members of the various teams were in the pews. It was an impressive send-off.

At the end of the Mass, before the

priests left the altar and the casket rolled back down the aisle by the six pallbearing coaches, Father Peter Rocca, rector of the basilica, stepped forward.

"Because of the inclement weather, the casket will not be accompanied to its final resting place by the congregation. The Nevilles ask that you say your final farewells outside the church. Those who wish are urged to join the Nevilles at the faculty club where luncheon will be served."

Looks of surprise were exchanged, but they were outnumbered by expressions of relief. A trudge through the still falling snow to Cedar Grove was not a prospect that appealed. Most of those in the church had been at the wake as well and could rightly feel that they had done their duty.

It had been deftly done, a first effort to deflect attention from the circumstances of Fred's death and forestall any scandal. It would have been premature to announce the suspicion of the police that Fred had not died from natural causes. The unstated assumption of the rector's announcement, for those who had ears to hear information that was not public, was that Fred was a suicide and the more quickly the results of the autopsy could be forgotten the better for the parents.

64

★ ★ ★

The post-funeral brunch at the faculty club was memorable for one thing. The grieving parents were already tiring of their role, the usual banalities had been expressed too many times, most were prepared to grab a bite and go. But the presence in the room of both Mary Shuster and Naomi McTear and the instinctive sense that there was a rivalry between the women that must eventually burst forth in words or action added a note of tension. Thus far the two women had not spoken to one another though it was apparent to Roger and he was certain to others as well that neither woman was ever unaware of the presence of the other. The immediate bone of contention had to do with the rights to the Nevilles. Mary had pride of place in the funeral home during the rosary, Naomi occupied the family pew at the Mass. Score, even. Who would manage to commandeer the Nevilles at the faculty club?

But Roger could not remain a spectator to the drama. Perhaps it was poor Marjorie's look of trepidation that decided him. He took up his vigil with the Nevilles, chattering away to one and the other, determined to stave off any incident. Phil had gone off with Jimmy Stewart, somewhat reluctantly missing the meal at the university club. It was a buffet and Roger followed the Nevilles through the line and guided them to a table. When they were seated, there was an empty chair. A problem. He levered himself to his feet and moved the chair against the wall, thus eliminating that all-too-inviting target for the two rivals.

"It was a lovely ceremony," Mrs. Neville said, her eyes damp.

"Good sermon," her husband said.

"That was Father Carmody."

And then, as if conjured into the room by mention of his name, Father Carmody appeared in the doorway. Roger rose and flayed his arms, attracting the priest's attention. Father Carmody's vision was not what it had been, and the room was filled with people, but it would have taken a blind man not to see Roger on his feet, churning his arms like a windmill. People stared. Eventually Father Carmody did too and he came to the table. As he approached, Roger retrieved the chair he had set against the wall and bowed Father Carmody into it.

"I don't have any food," the priest said.

"Sit still. I'll fetch some for you."

And off he went to the buffet table, navigating through the crowd like an errant linebacker. Against all his principles, he went to the head of the line and began filling a plate.

"For Father Carmody," he explained to the world at large. He repeated the explanation several times before turning and seeing with dismay that Mary Shuster had taken the chair he had vacated. Naomi McTear was entering the room from the bar, a Bloody Mary in her hand. Her eyes met Roger's and then by a fated triangulation they both looked at Mary. Naomi's eyes sparked and she started across the room. Roger, balancing the plate of food for Father Carmody, headed for the table. The vector of their approaches narrowed but Roger, despite his bulk, got to the table first and, as he served Father Carmody, interposed his enormous bulk between Naomi and the table. She would have to circumnavigate him in order to have a scene. Mary was deep in conversation with Mrs. Neville, the subject Fred.

"It was our secret," she was saying. "I didn't even tell my mother. Not yet. You know why we thought it wiser to wait to announce our engagement."

Mrs. Neville looked utterly bewildered at

this remark. The source of her bewilderment then appeared, successfully getting around Roger's bulk.

"Have you met Naomi?" Mrs. Neville cried. She looked desperately at her husband. His hearing was not what it had been and was further impeded by the expensive hearing aid he wore. He was explaining the theory of the device to Father Carmody, who might have caught every other word, his own hearing not what it was. Besides, the background noise was the classic instance of what could make a hearing aid fail. The intricacies of Mr. Neville's digital device fascinated Father Carmody. Neville popped it from his ear and handed it to Father Carmody. The priest drew back as if reluctant to handle so complicated and expensive a piece of equipment.

"An ear horn would work better," Neville said.

Father Carmody was surprised by this, having just heard Neville explain how the device had been programmed to correct the precise weaknesses in his hearing, that it was a veritable little computer in itself, adjusting to changes in the circumambient acoustical situation.

"You're not satisfied with it?"

"You know what digital hearing aids are?" He paused and then stuck a digit into both ears and grinned. Father Carmody's barking laugh rewarded him and he beamed. An observer might have thought that Neville was stopping his ears to some communication from Carmody. Roger took all this in in the interval between Mrs. Neville's acknowledgment of the arrival of Naomi and that young lady's response.

"I was Fred's fiancée," Naomi said. She switched her drink to the other hand and extended the free one to Mary.

"Yes. I know you were. Fred told me all about it."

"It was hardly a secret."

Mrs. Neville glanced furtively at Mary, whose claim had been characterized as secret.

"No," Mary said. "Nor that he had broken the engagement."

"Broken!" Naomi glared at Mary and then thrust forth the hand on which the massive diamond was all too visible. "Haven't you noticed this?"

"I know all about that."

"I love your dress," Naomi said.

"It's what one wears in mourning."

Naomi was expensively clothed in a bright dress of subdued floral pattern, a

69

very short skirt and a long jacket. The height of her heels was a marvel to Roger. His eye caught Marjorie's and he beckoned her to the table, hoping that in numbers there would be an impediment to an open quarrel.

"Haven't I seen you on television?" Father Carmody asked Naomi.

Her anger fled and she smiled brightly at the priest. "I do sideline color on television."

"At football games?"

"Yes."

"An odd job for a woman."

The smiled disappeared. "People used to think so."

Marjorie arrived and looked anxiously at the others. Roger explained to Naomi who she was.

"Ah. Miss Havisham's mother."

At that Father Carmody launched into an account of a woman sports reporter who had insisted on gaining entry to the locker room where players in various stages of undress had understandably taken her presence to be provocative. Things were said, parts of her anatomy were patted, she fled.

"Then she had the effrontery to bring suit against the players," Father Carmody said with disgust. "For being in their birthday suits, I guess."

Naomi's chin lifted and she looked frostily at the priest. It did not help that Mary decided to break her mourning by bursting into laughter. Naomi left them, moving majestically across the room. Others recognized her and soon she was the object of adulation.

"Bless you, Father," Mary said.

"For I have sinned?"

3   Fred Neville's apartment was a surprise — sparsely furnished with very modern furniture, a contour chair over which a futuristic lamp craned like a tropical bird, on one wall a large canvas covered with streaks of primary colors, a couch that was little more than a slab of leather randomly covered with a dozen pillows. Another tropical bird looked down on it. The carpet was plush, greenish, the walls chalk white. When Phil and Jimmy Stewart checked out the bedroom they found an austere room. A single bed, one chair, a lamp affixed to the wall over the bed in which Fred's body had been found. Chalk-white walls here too, but no pictures. It was a relief to go into the study.

Here there was clutter and dozens of unmatching colors, pictures Scotch-taped to the walls, one a photograph of Lilac House, apparently taken by Fred himself. And books, books everywhere, books on shelves, books in piles, books beside the old-fashioned easy chair and on the footstool in front of it. The desk seemed to be a trestle table but its nature was obscured by the burden it bore — a computer, a printer, a fax machine. There were piles of paper on it and beneath it stacks of magazines. The chair before the computer was a stenographer's chair, armless, firm back support. Messages were taped to the computer and to the walls. Even Jimmy Stewart seemed relieved by the study's contrast with the other rooms in the apartment.

"What are we looking for?" Phil asked.

"If we knew, we wouldn't be here. Let's start with the notes."

Most of them were reminders to do things on dates that had long since passed. There was a fax message in the basket of the machine. Jimmy Stewart looked at it and then passed it to Phil without comment.

Isadore of Seville loved etymology,
Loved to analyse the source of words,
Or invented them without apology,
Visigoths and others with their herds
Exchanged their tongues for Latin,
  more or less,
Mixing barbarian dialects with it.
Ancient authors always had the wit,
Received, then polished, with which they
  could express
Young thoughts in language old.

73

Soon the wine was watered, the language
  bastardized,
Harsh sounds, with meanings harsh with
  northern cold,
Upset the tongue that Virgil standardized.
Subject to invasion like the empire,
True Latin, having risen, fell.
Eventually in Seville our Isadore
Reverently misread the words in his
  provincial cell.

Jimmy Stewart watched Phil as he read it. "What do you make of that?"

"I'm no judge."

"Did you notice the sender?"

The message was from Fred Neville as well as to him. Phil shrugged.

"What's a sports guy doing collecting stuff like that?"

"At least he didn't send it to someone else."

"I don't suppose it matters where he found it."

"We can ask Roger."

Phil made a copy of it on the machine that emerged from beneath a pile of paper, folded it and put it in the jacket pocket of his good suit.

The two men went systematically through the items in the study, read old fax messages, none of them poetic, all from senders other than Fred. Often they were acknowledgments of data he had sent reporters, Notre Dame statistics to facilitate reporting of a game. From time to time, one showed something to the other. Phil passed a fax to Stewart from Naomi McTear, acknowledging receipt of such statistics.

"What's that mean?" Stewart pointed to the final line: *XOXOXOXO.*

Phil thought about it. "Those are the letters used to diagram plays."

"This one make any sense?"

"Maybe the *X*'s represent the defense and the O's the offense."

"Maybe."

"It doesn't read like a message from his fiancée."

"Business," Jimmy Stewart said.

And they got back to business. It was difficult to know why Fred had kept most of the papers stacked on the desk and scattered on the floor around it. He seemed never to have thrown anything away. Of course they went through all the books, looking for anything Fred might have inserted in them. There were stubs from airline tickets, a holy card depicting Blessed Brother André, the holy man who had lived a life of obscurity in Montreal whom the Congregation of Holy Cross was hoping to get canonized, another of a youthful Pope John XXIII. A postcard from Fred's parents when they had been on a Carribean cruise. Nothing at all relevant to his death. Some hours after they had entered the study, only the computer was left. Neither man trusted himself to check it out.

"Would Roger do it?"

"He'd probably ask Greg Whelan to come with him."

"That's good enough for me. But it should be done fairly soon."

From the kitchen they took the canister of sugar as well as the sugar bowl on the table where Fred had taken his solitary meals when he ate at home. The refrigerator was full of TV dinners and other microwaveable goodies. And lots of beer.

"Care for one?"

"I don't suppose it could be called destroying evidence."

"Not by me."

Jimmy Stewart decided to put a bag of popcorn in the microwave and when he popped open the door there was a wallet lying on the round tray. He found a kind of tongs in a drawer, extracted the wallet and dropped it in a baggie.

"That explains why there was no wallet in his trousers."

"Was he dressed when he was found?"

"I thought you knew that."

They sat at the kitchen table, drank beer, and went over what they knew about Fred Neville's death, which wasn't much. He hadn't shown up at his office for a few days but no one seemed surprised at first.

"I wonder if he took days off regularly," Jimmy Stewart said.

"You can ask."

"I will."

After Fred had failed to show up at his office for three days, Roger had been induced to check on Fred and was let into the apartment after explaining the concern of the Notre Dame athletic department. Roger's first reaction had been to think Fred had suffered a youthful heart attack, or perhaps had some illness he'd never mentioned. A diabetic might slip away while in a coma. Because of the length of time from Fred's failing to show up at his office and the discovery of the body, an autopsy was made. Traces of poison had shown up in Fred's system, sufficient to account for his death.

"Did he have any enemies?" Jimmy asked.

"Everybody liked Fred," Phil said.

"Meaning you and Roger did."

"Ask anybody in the athletic department."

"I'll ask everybody in the athletic department."

"They'll tell you. He was just a guy people liked."

"So it was suicide."

"I would never believe that. Fred was a devout Catholic."

"And that rules out suicide. Are you ever loyal."

"Loyal? I'm not a Catholic."

"You're not?" Stewart was surprised. Did he think everybody was Catholic?

"Roger is a convert. He's the Catholic in the family."

"But you're so gung-ho Notre Dame."

"That makes me a Catholic?"

"An honorary one at least."

The building manager, a man named Santander, had an apartment in the basement of the building. He was in his sixties, bald but with hair sprouting from his ears and nostrils, and unhappy to be disturbed. Behind him in the apartment a television roared. Jimmy Stewart identified himself and Santander became cooperative.

"Come in, come in."

It was a snug little place he had, redolent of garlic and pepper. A Notre Dame blanket was thrown over the beat-up couch.

"What do you pay for this place?" Stewart asked.

"Pay? I'm the manager. This is one of the perks of the job."

"Free rent? I hope you declare it on your income tax. That would come to quite a sum each year."

"Income tax! I thought you were city police."

"We're investigating the death of Fred Neville."

Santander waved them to twin beat-up chairs and sat on the edge of the couch. "What a great guy he was."

"You liked him?"

"Everybody liked him. See this blanket? He gave me this."

"Better report that too."

"Hey, stop that."

Jimmy Stewart stopped it. He began to ask Santander about the days before Fred's body was found. The manager shrugged.

"Nothing. I didn't see him but, what the heck, he could have been on the road."

"Anyone visit him?"

"You mean the big fat guy?"

"He discovered the body. I mean before that."

"No one but his girl. And don't even think it. She never stayed over."

"You check on such things?"

"I just know it."

Phil said, "His girl. Always the same one."

"Of course. They were in love."

"What was her name?"

"She worked at Notre Dame too. Mary. Mary something. You could look it up."

"We will," Jimmy Stewart said.

4 Griselda Novak had never personally known someone who died, not before Fred Neville, but even so she was ashamed that all she seemed to want to do was consider the effect of his death on her. She remembered glimpses of him around the Joyce Athletic and Convocation Center, she remembered him on trips with the Lady Irish to games away from campus, but most of all she remembered the dinner she'd had with him at Parisi's when he had been assigned to talk her out of leaving the team. Would that evening had been so etched in her memory if Fred were still alive? After all, it had been talking with Professor Knight that had changed her mind, not anything Fred had said. But she had sensed that he, like herself, aspired to be like Roger Knight.

When he had taken her unannounced to the Knight brothers' apartment, she had sensed that their entrance created something of a sensation, at least with Mary Shuster. Of course Griselda knew that there was something between Mary and Fred — she supposed everyone connected with Notre Dame sports knew about it —

but when they came in, Mary gave Fred the cold shoulder, and Griselda realized it was because Fred had taken her to dinner. The woman was jealous! Griselda had to admit she had enjoyed that, incredible as the suspicion had been. Fred was so much older than she that it had never occurred to her that anyone would imagine they had been on a date.

It was a little much, though, for Mary to show up at the wake and funeral clad all in black, calling attention to herself and away from Fred. And then the woman named Naomi showed up and turned out to be Fred's fiancée. It had made Griselda curious to learn what exactly Mary's relation to Fred had been. She had certainly been upstaged by Naomi. What Griselda found hard to believe was that either woman had really cared for Fred. And wasn't it sick to be fighting over a dead man?

At the get-together at the university club Griselda became aware that she was the only member of the team there. Not even Muffin had come from the church to the club. But once she was there she decided to say. For one thing, she was hungry. For another, Roger Knight was there. So she witnessed the little scene at the table where Roger had been sitting with Fred's parents.

She saw Mary take his seat when Roger went to get the old priest some food. And then Naomi showed up at the table and it looked as if there would be a catfight. But the old priest seemed to put a stop to that and Naomi walked away. Griselda watched her showing off to those who crowded around her and drew near. Someone turned, a man with a silly expression that got sillier when he saw her.

"Griselda! Hey look, Griselda Novak is here."

The circle re-formed around her, with Naomi McTear a member of it, no longer the center. Griselda had a sweet feeling of revenge, for what she didn't know, but she did like these fans to be fussing over her rather than the sidelines color reporter from cable television.

"Griselda is the guard of the half century," the man with the silly expression said to Naomi.

"I love to watch you play," Naomi said.

"It's only a game."

Everyone laughed. Is this the way people behaved after a funeral? But then look at herself, trying to score points against Naomi. The reporter did have a way of flashing her great big diamond.

"You're right," Naomi said. "Most of

you have lost a friend. I have lost the man I intended to marry."

The circle re-formed and Griselda slipped away. It was difficult to say who was worse, Naomi or Mary.

"You knew Fred, didn't you?"

Griselda turned, and there was Mary Shuster.

"Of course."

"You play basketball."

"In my spare time."

Under her black mantilla, Mary's face softened. "We met at the Knights' apartment."

"I remember."

"You came in with Fred."

"We'd been to dinner at Parisi's."

"Did you do a lot of that?"

"Not enough. But don't tell his fiancée."

"She isn't, you know."

"Her diamond could have fooled me."

"It's meant to."

"She isn't his fiancée?"

"It's a long story."

"You'll have to tell me sometime."

"How about now? I want to go home and change out of this dress."

"You're through mourning?"

Tears formed in Mary's eyes and ran down her cheeks. She turned away.

"Please. I'm sorry. I shouldn't have said that."

Mary shrugged. Griselda took her arm and guided her through the room to the front lobby of the club.

"I'll go with you. I want to hear all about it."

When they came outside, Griselda asked, "Is your car here?"

"Oh, we can walk. We live in Harter Heights."

Griselda looked blank.

"It's just off Angela Boulevard."

They set off. Most of the snow had melted now and as they passed Cedar Grove, Griselda said, "Isn't it odd that we didn't accompany the body to the cemetery?"

"Not in the circumstances."

"I don't understand."

"Then you haven't heard. They fear that Fred's death was not due to natural causes."

"No!"

Was this among the things that Mary had offered to tell her? They went on in silence while Griselda contemplated the implications of Mary's astounding remark. The sun was shining fitfully but a stiff breeze was in their faces when they turned onto Angela.

"It's not far," Mary said, raising her voice against the wind.

Griselda nodded and ducked her head. Not due to natural causes. What did that mean? And then the grim thought occurred and she wondered if she really wanted to hear more. But, whatever the phrase meant, it was certain to become public sooner or later and she wanted to learn now what it meant. How discreet Father Rocca's words now seemed in light of Mary's remark. It was not the sort of thing one would want to announce from the altar after the funeral Mass.

The Shuster house looked like something from an old magazine. Mary opened the unlocked door and they went inside, hung up their coats, and headed to the kitchen where Mary proceeded to put on coffee.

"What a lovely house."

"I've lived here all my life. This area used to be the favored spot for faculty. All our neighbors were professors when I was young."

"Your father too?"

"Oh, yes." Mary smiled wryly. "It is a lesson in something or other the way people who were prominent at the university are so swiftly forgotten when they are gone."

The kitchen was old-fashioned but cheerful, with what was called a breakfast nook instead of table and chairs. Griselda slid onto a bench.

"I'll show you the house later if you'd like. My mother should be home by then. Now we can just talk."

And so they did, with coffee mugs before them. Griselda sensed that Mary needed to talk more than she herself needed to listen.

"You must have noticed that Fred and I were very much in love."

"When you visited him at the Joyce Center."

She nodded. "We saw no need to hide it there. Now I am paying the penalty of our decision to keep our engagement a secret."

"Why did you do that?"

"Two reasons. First, my mother. She is an incorrigible matchmaker and has been pushing me at men for years. When finally I met Fred and we fell in love, I wanted to keep it from her for a time. I suppose I was fearful that her reaction would be trium- phant, finally getting her old-maid daughter off her hands."

"Old maid!"

"I think my mother thought she was stuck with me forever. Of course I exag- gerate."

"What was the other reason for keeping it secret?"

"That was Fred's. When he told Naomi he wanted to break their engagement, she wouldn't accept it. I guess she was quite angry and threatening. She said she would sue him for breach of promise."

"In this day and age?"

"It does sound somewhat Victorian, doesn't it? But he wanted time for her to get used to the fact and accept that they were no longer engaged."

Griselda thought of the woman who strode away from the table where Roger Knight had been sitting with Father Carmody and the Nevilles. When she went to talk to the Nevilles, Mary had assumed the chair Roger had temporarily vacated.

"I thought you were going to fight at the club."

"You can see what a forceful personality she has. She would have dropped Fred without hesitation if she had wanted to, but she could not accept being dropped."

"She wouldn't give back the ring."

"Oh, that is her mother's."

"Her mother's!"

Mary nodded. "She gave it to herself. Anyway, those are the reasons we never announced it. And why I am now in such a peculiar position."

Mary still wore her mourning dress, apparently having forgotten her intention to change.

"What did you mean when you said 'not by natural causes'," asked Griselda.

Mary held her mug in both hands and for a moment stared into it. When she looked at Griselda, there were tears in her eyes.

"I blame Naomi. If she would have accepted the end of their engagement, he would not have been so torn. I didn't realize how difficult she had made life for him. He was in a cruel dilemma. On the one hand, he had a fiancée he no longer loved, perhaps he never had, but she would not let him go. On the other hand, the woman he loved. He must have crumbled under the pressure."

"Suicide?" Griselda whispered the word.

Mary sobbed. "Worse than having him gone is the thought that I should have done something to prevent it."

"You had no inkling?"

"Only in retrospect. But not at the time." She wiped her eyes. "He had an older sister who died in mysterious circumstances. Perhaps she was a suicide too."

Griselda almost wished she hadn't come but of course what she really wished was that what she had heard could not be so.

5   In 1963 when what was then called the Memorial Library was opened — only later was it named after the longtime president of the university, Father Theodore Hesburgh — the university archives had been assigned the sixth floor, a space that had seemed ample at the time. But the accumulation of archival materials, plus the exponential increase in the number of volumes that caused the library to covet the space, seemed to make it inevitable that someday new quarters would have to be found for the archives. But crowded though it was, and accessible by way of an unassuming single door just to the right of the elevators, those who worked there had come to cherish their working conditions, and none more so than Greg Whelan. Of course the jammed condition made it difficult to accommodate such visitors as Roger Knight, but then Roger presented a problem wherever he went.

On the afternoon of the funeral, Greg had commandeered one of the rooms in the archives set aside for visiting scholars, and it was there behind a closed door that he and Roger discussed the strange passing of their mutual friend, Fred Neville.

"There seem to be two young ladies who expected Fred to marry them," Roger said.

"I never noticed anything between Fred and Mary."

"How often did we see them together?"

"Not often."

"Almost never, Greg. But Griselda led me to believe that at the Joyce Center the two of them were what gossip columnists call an item."

"It's odd how the meaning of that word developed."

"Which one?"

"*Item*. Literally, it means *again*. In lists it prefaced different points, functioning much like *a, b, c*. Then it came to mean the contents of what it introduced. So what was listed became an item."

Roger listened with pleasure. He always came away from a visit with Greg with some, well, item of information which, whether it came as complete news or not, was welcome. Silently, he shared Greg's delight that with Roger he could be fluent, no trace of his stammer. His little linguistic aside was preparatory to what they had meant to discuss.

"At first it was possible to imagine that Mary had merely imagined her liaison with

Fred. Not so, if Griselda is right, as I'm sure she is."

"But wearing black!"

"Her mother knew nothing of it either, Greg."

"Of what?"

"The fact that Mary and Fred intended to marry."

"That doesn't seem like a motive for suicide," Greg said, with a sly smile. Among bachelors a certain amount of misogyny is de rigueur.

"But it is Naomi McTear who has a diamond ring and who is accepted by the Nevilles as their future daughter-in-law."

"She looks like a tough cookie."

"A liberated woman?"

"Enslaved by her job. I don't know what Fred saw in her."

"Phil says she is stunning."

"So is novocaine."

"Phil knows such things."

A moment of silence during which the two seemed to acknowledge that they did not.

Greg said, "I had the feeling that Mrs. Shuster was measuring Phil for the role of son-in-law."

"After she saw I wouldn't do."

"Really?"

"Phil says so."

The ensuing silence lasted more than a minute. Greg seemed to decide that there was no adequate comment he could make.

"Fred came here a couple of times to examine the materials we have on Maurice Francis Egan."

"A man of varied interests."

"A mystery man."

"Everyone is a mystery."

Roger loved the archives and sometimes envied Greg the life he led among the boxes and boxes of Notre Dame lore. It was an odd thought that the present would one day be the past and matters of seemingly fleeting moment now be represented here in bits and pieces for some future scholar to make sense of. Doubtless Greg would start a file on Fred Neville and his untimely demise. The fact that the death was no longer ascribed to natural causes made this almost a certainty.

"Poison?" Greg asked.

"So Jimmy Stewart says."

"Self-administered?"

Roger's expression became pained. "They have to examine every possibility."

"He had no enemies, did he?"

"So far as I know, everybody liked him. And two women loved him enough to want to be his wife."

"You have to keep me posted on the investigation."

"Of course."

That night Phil told Roger of the examination of Fred's apartment. He had changed into comfortable clothing — Levis, a Notre Dame sweatshirt, loafers — and was sitting in a kitchen chair watching Roger prepare their evening meal.

"Phil, it can't be suicide."

"Probably not. At any rate, he had a visitor during the days he was missing from his office."

"Who?"

"Mary Shuster."

"Surely there is nothing suspicious in that, given what we now know."

"What we know is what Mary tells us."

"Are you saying that Jimmy Stewart suspects Mary?"

"He intends to interview her."

6   The University of Notre Dame is the nine-hundred-pound gorilla in the South Bend area. The largest local employer, it is the reason 95 percent of visitors come to South Bend, the target of eighty thousand fans at every home football game when the local police are pressed into service to direct the influx of automobiles, vans, SUVs, and their excited occupants. Whenever a police matter involves the university, the local constabulary proceeds with consummate diplomacy, not wanting to offend Notre Dame officials, willing to keep under wraps things that would normally be splashed across the pages of the local paper. Jimmy Stewart did not object to this. In many ways it made such work as he did easier, justifying keeping the media in the dark. So it was with the case of Fred Neville.

That the assistant sports information director should have been found dead in his apartment after being absent without leave for days was already something not to make a fuss about. Such things happen. But Boswell the coroner had complicated matters with the results of his autopsy.

"He died of poisoning." Boswell seemed to take a lugubrious pleasure in telling Jimmy Stewart this. But then he was a Purdue graduate. Boswell was thin and wore a toupee, which in the ads that had convinced him to buy it promised a return to youth and an enhancement of appearance. Stewart wondered if Boswell really believed his hairpiece wouldn't be recognized as such from anywhere within five hundred yards. Reddish and lush, it sat atop his head in such a way that it immediately called attention to itself. It had sideburns that stood out from the head except where the bows of Boswell's glasses gripped them, seemingly keeping the thing in place.

"You're sure?"

Boswell was sure. That had sent Jimmy Stewart to the apartment where he took possession of the cup on the stand beside the bed in which Fred had been found. Boswell soon reported that he had found in the cup traces of the same poison he had found in the body.

"Suicide?"

Boswell had shrugged. "I have no way to tell. Of course I can't rule it out. It would be much simpler, wouldn't it."

This was a crack at the special treatment

Notre Dame received from the police in delicate matters.

After the funeral, Jimmy Stewart and Phil Knight had gone through the apartment. It was filled with stuff but nothing cast much light on what had happened to Neville. They might have been spared a lot of time if they had gone to the manager of the building first. The fact that he had seen Mary Shuster visit Fred meant that she was probably the last person to have seen him alive.

A call at the Shuster home the following morning brought a somewhat bedraggled Mrs. Shuster to the door, wrapped in a housecoat, edgy and unwelcoming. It did not help much when Jimmy Stewart identified himself.

"I am going to pay that ticket, for heaven's sake. I'll do it today."

"I'm not in traffic, Mrs. Shuster. I want to talk to you about Fred Neville."

"Fred Neville? God rest his soul. Can't you let him lie in peace?" The question raised another in her mind. "But he isn't buried yet, is he?"

"That's what I want to talk to you about."

Either Mary was home or she was not. If not, Mrs. Shuster was an attractive target of opportunity. He had piqued her curiosity and she opened the door.

Stewart was struck by the decisively male note of the furnishings and decorations of the house. The living room walls were hung with certificates, awards, degrees, all honoring the late Nathaniel Shuster. The dining room seemed an anteroom to the study beyond, a book-lined room well-lit by a skylight.

"What a wonderful house."

"This is an area of wonderful houses. But no longer of wonderful people. No, I shouldn't say that. What I mean is that it is no longer filled with members of the faculty and their families. Of course the whole city has changed."

Stewart nodded. Everyone had a right to a certain number of philosophical generalizations.

"How long has your husband been dead, Mrs. Shuster?"

"You haven't told me your name."

He got out his identification again, and she gave a wave of her hand. "You don't think I could read that, do you?"

"My name is Jimmy Stewart. Detective Lieutenant Jimmy Stewart, South Bend police. I am making inquiries about the death of Fred Neville."

She listened as if he were reciting a set lesson. "Very well. My husband has been dead fifteen years." And to his look of surprise as he again looked around him, she added, "It is exactly as it was the day he died. I will never change it. I suppose that is why I stay on here while so many others have left. It would be like deserting Nathaniel."

"I understand."

"Now what do you mean, looking into the death of Fred Neville."

"You knew him, of course."

"I thought I did."

Stewart lifted his brows and looked receptive.

"My daughter now tells me that she had been seeing Fred, that they intended to marry. I knew absolutely nothing of this."

"She was engaged to Neville?"

Mrs. Shuster nodded. "So you know of the fiancée who showed up for the funeral."

"Naomi McTear?"

"Yes. The Nevilles obviously accepted her as their son's fiancée, which put Mary in an equivocal position, to say the least. I don't suppose you were there."

"Yes, I was."

"I thought I had seen you somewhere.

You were at the wake too, weren't you?"

"That's right."

"The young woman dressed in mourning was my daughter, not the fiancée. Oh, I am so mortified."

"If your daughter and Neville were seeing one another, others must have known. You don't imagine she just invented such a relationship, do you?"

"I don't know what to think." She stopped. "Why are the police asking about Fred Neville's death?"

"At first, it was thought he died of natural causes."

"Didn't he!"

"His death was due to poison."

"Oh my God." She brought both hands to her face and stared round-eyed at him over her fingertips. After a moment, she took her hands away to ask eagerly, "Did he leave a note?"

"None has been found."

"Oh, you must look for it. For anything that could indicate what was going on between him and Mary."

"You say Mary herself gave you no clue?" He looked toward the stairs. "I assume she isn't home."

"Oh, she was off to work, bright as a penny this morning."

"Where does she work?"

"In the registrar's office."

"On campus."

"Of course. And no, she gave me no clue. And I can add this. I have looked through her room, her things, for anything that would prove she wasn't living some fantasy."

"And?"

"Nothing. Absolutely nothing. That is why I would so much like you to find a note from him."

"Mrs. Shuster, it may not have been suicide."

She fell back in her chair, but bounced upright again, the cushions were so firm.

"What do you mean?"

"There could have been foul play. We have no evidence of that but in the absence of a note or any indication that the man was despondent . . ."

"You think he might have been killed."

A look of horror spread across Mrs. Shuster's face. "Is that why you came here? Are you thinking that Mary —"

Jimmy Stewart interrupted her. "I'm not paid to think, not in that sense. Mary can be of great help to us in finding out what happened. If there had not been an autopsy, if the coroner had not found poison to be the cause of death — either or both of which might easily not have happened — Fred Neville would be safely in the ground and we could all go about our usual work. But there was an autopsy and poison was found and it is my job to discover what that means. Was it suicide or something else? Mary will know things that will help me answer that question."

Her expression changed gradually during this explanation, and she was wary of him now. He changed gears.

"I have been noticing the study ever since I sat down, Mrs. Shuster. I wonder if I could have a closer look at it."

"Of course!"

She had trouble getting out of the chair and he helped her and they went arm and arm through the dining room to the living room.

Close up, the study seemed even more a stage setting than it had from the living room. Jimmy Stewart started to move along the shelves, then turned. "May I?"

"Oh, do. Eventually these books will go to the Notre Dame library, a special collection, the Professor Nathaniel Shuster collection, but I could no more part with them than I could with the house."

"What was your husband's field?"

"Political science. But his real love was American literature."

"And these are his own works." He was looking at a special shelf.

"The books yes. I mean to have the offprints of his articles bound. They will make at least four volumes."

"Very productive scholar."

"He was a poet too."

"Really."

"He said he wrote them just for me, or Mary, but I sent some of them off and they were accepted." She pulled a slender volume from the shelf. *Poems* by Nathaniel Shuster. "This is the result. It doesn't seem much, does it? But poetry takes a very long time to write. And rewrite. It was very difficult for him to think that a version was the final one."

Stewart held his peace. They were moving into terra incognita as far as he was concerned, but he now felt Mrs. Shuster to be a far more sympathetic character than he had. Her indignation was motivated by fear of what people would think or say but on the topic of her husband, on the devotion she still felt to him and the life they had lived together, she emerged as a warm and sentimental woman. No doubt Mary's enigmatic actions had jarred with what lay behind this shrine of a house, and it was that, her husband's memory, that was the true measure of her indignation.

They moved back through the rooms and Stewart thanked her for her time.

"Would you like me to call Mary and tell her you're coming?"

"No. I want to stop by a friend's apartment on the way. Philip Knight."

Mrs. Shuster stepped back, her hands lifting in delighted surprise.

"You know Philip Knight?"

"And Roger."

"Why didn't you say so, for heaven's sake? They are both dear friends of mine."

"I will give them your regards."

7   South Bend is ringed with motels, with the greatest concentration to the north and east, particularly the east, where the area around the mall is dotted with motels, inns, and hotels. Their number was explained by the influx of fans for home games, hardly a sufficient basis for yearlong profit, but somehow the number of guests through the year made it a paying proposition. There were condominium apartments as well, which waited empty for the return of alumni and benefactors of the university. The cable company for which Naomi McTear worked had several such apartments and it was in one of these that she was staying. Indeed, her presence for Fred's funeral was explained by the fact that she had been assigned to a Lady Irish home game.

"Lady Irish?" Like most successful women she took a dim view of women, and sometimes she thought that it was only former coaches who took women athletes seriously. Heresy, of course, never to be voiced aloud or indicated in tone or manner. Gender equality was a demanding game, most of whose rules were written ad hoc, and it was dangerously easy to over-step some invisible line and be declared a traitor to her sex.

Naomi's interest in sports was entirely theoretical, a matter of knowledge rather than practice. She was an only daughter whose older brother, George, had excelled at every sport he had undertaken. George was now in his forties and paying the be-lated price for having being banged around on the gridiron in college and the pros. He was wracked with arthritis, had two new knees, moved with great deliberateness using a cane and, finding the pain-control pills inadequate, had sought solace in drink. From time to time he was inter-viewed and the results now were invariably embarrassing. Her brother Tom was an-other story entirely, one of the voices of the Chicago Cubs as well as the Bulls. It was Tom on whom she had modeled her life. He was inept at sports but his head was filled with lore that was ever at his finger-tips, a great asset in his trade. If George could do it, Tom knew it, and George had always deferred to his young brother in the matter of sports statistics. Knowledge is power. Naomi had vowed to become a fe-male version of Tom.

And she had. She had written sports in

college, had devoted more time to absorbing histories of sports, first the major ones, then all the others. By the time she graduated, she was a walking encyclopedia. When she met Fred Neville it was like attracting like. The first time she sat in on one of his postgame performances with the media she recognized a kindred spirit. She asked a question about pre-Rockne football and he rattled off the answer and looked at her with renewed interest. After the news conference she asked him to dinner.

"I have an expense account," she explained. "Besides I want to know you better."

Directness is the best direction to take with men, as long as it is done in a matter-of-fact, nonthreatening way. Fred accepted, he suggested the Carriage House and as they drove, she was sure he had lost the way. But suddenly, in the middle of nowhere was this excellent restaurant.

"I don't suppose you drink," she said.

"Don't you?"

"That depends."

"On what?"

"On whether you do."

They started with a scotch and water and had a bottle of cabernet with their meal. And talked. And talked. They were taking the other's measure, and it was like a parlor game. Baseball? They both knew baseball like the back of their hand. Football, of course, and basketball. And so on through the roll of sports and each might have been talking to himself rather than the other. Fred could have been a clone of Tom.

"He's your brother? I should have known."

"Why?"

"You have the same command of your subject."

They were among the last diners to rise and go. Outside it was a lovely fall evening and high above them stars were visible in a clear sky. And it was so quiet.

"You all right?" she asked when they got to his car.

"I'm the designated hitter."

"Then I hope you strike out."

The words hung there in the silent air, meaning more than she intended. It was the first thing either had said that suggested that he was male and she female. Scoring and striking out took on new meanings.

The moment passed, they got in, and he drove with great care back to South Bend.

"My treat next time," he said when he dropped her off.

"Wasn't this time a treat?"

"In every sense."

That had been several years ago, during the Bob Davie years. Naomi had angled to get her assignments changed, but it was difficult to get Notre Dame games, since so many others wanted them. But she got more than her share and each time she was in town she and Fred got together. The intervals gave Naomi time to think what it was leading to, if anything. But first Fred had to be introduced to Tom. This was arranged and the three of them got together for a postgame dinner to discuss the incredible loss the Irish had just suffered because they had let the clock run out when they were on the opponent's six-yard line. A field goal would have given them victory. They had a time-out left. But the clock was allowed to run and a confused squad left the field in defeat.

What Naomi had expected to happen did not happen. Tom had not liked Fred. Of course, Tom was drinking, the family weakness, and became surly as the dinner progressed. If the nation is divided into those who love Notre Dame and those who hate her, it became clear that Tom fell among the latter. His criticisms of the school, particularly of the treatment of its teams by the national media, began as humorous asides, and might have been directed against Naomi and her colleagues on national television, but as the meal progressed, the humor receded and bitterness was unmasked. And Fred's defense turned from being lighthearted deflection of criticism he spent much of his professional life hearing to being serious, an artillery barrage of statistics, with a recurrent mention of the percentage of athletes who actually graduated, a most impressive statistic indeed. But not to Tom.

"So you have a cadre of soft professors who take it easy on the jocks."

"We do not. Nor are there any bogus majors in basket weaving or physical education. Check it out."

The success of the teams? As even the rah-rah tradition acknowledged, it was largely a matter of luck. Nor were the schedules played as demanding as other schools faced. And of course, like the Yankees — Tom hated the Yankees — Notre Dame could buy any coach they wanted and lure to the campus any athlete.

Again and again, realizing what a mistake she had made, Naomi tried to get the conversation on other matters, but it was far too late for that.

"Oh, Tom, for heaven's sake."

"Oh, Tom, for heaven's sake," he echoed, mimicking her tone. She could have hit him. He was her favorite brother, the one she was almost desperate should like Fred, and he was behaving like this!

Eventually, as happened when he drank, Tom passed into a further bibulous phase, from argumentative to sentimental. It was not welcome. He decided to tell Fred what a wonderful sister he had.

"It's why I never married. Where could I find someone like her?"

"Oh, Tom."

He did not mimic her. She almost wished he had. He became moist-eyed, reminding her of their idyllic childhood, about their sainted mother. Throughout all this, Naomi had avoided meeting Fred's eyes. She knew what his reaction must be. The talk about marriage was too much. She went off to the Ladies and stared at her face in the mirror. She saw there a woman in the cruel position of having to choose between her favorite brother — and there was, after all, Tom sober to offset the awfulness of Tom drunk — and Fred

Neville. But did she have the choice after this? Fred had been attentive, he obviously liked her, but what would he think of any future that involved a relationship with Tom?

But when she returned to the table, Tom had entered into the final, good-humored endearing stage. He and Fred were in happy conversation. They had agreed on the immortal status of Joe Paterno, which was insufficiently acknowledged by the sportswriting fraternity. "And sorority," Tom added as she joined them.

If it were only this final effect drink had on Tom, Naomi would have welcomed his drinking. The evening ended on a high note.

"Let's have an Irish coffee," Tom said.

It seemed a peace offering. They all three had Irish coffee, a drink Naomi liked about as much as she liked eggnog. Outside, they put Tom in a cab and Naomi turned to face Fred.

"That wasn't what I planned," she said.

"It was fun," he said, his tone false.

"I'll make it up to you." Impulsively, she lifted her face and kissed him. Almost to her surprise, he took her in his arms in a crushing embrace and pressed his lips more firmly on hers.

If that dinner with Tom had been the result of a plan, it would have been successful so far as its ultimate outcome. They ended up at her suite where a somewhat woozy Fred, collapsed in a chair, took off his tie and kicked off his shoes.

"I haven't had that much to drink in a long time."

"Me either. Or is it, neither have I? Or is it, can I get you anything?"

He had put back his head and his eyes were at half-mast.

"Don't fall asleep!"

"I don't even remember driving here."

Naomi looked down at him in silence. Then she took his hands, heaved him to his feet, and led him down the hall to the bedroom.

During the week, she got a call from Tom.

"I hope you're not serious about that guy."

"I'm surprised you remember him."

"You better forget him too."

8 When Phil suggested that the three of them have lunch on campus while they talked, Mary frowned.

"I'd like to get away, if you don't mind."

Perhaps she did not want those she worked with to see her being interviewed by the police.

Jimmy Stewart said, "I'm surprised you came to work."

"It was either that or stay home."

"I talked with your mother this morning."

"Oh, Lord." She looked at Phil, as if he would understand the remark. Was she referring to her mother's clumsy efforts to pair herself and Phil?

Jimmy Stewart suggested the Mikado on 31, a splendid restaurant that had not yet been discovered by avid lunch goers. The menu was varied, the service suggestive of geisha deference, the dining room a clean well-lighted place. Phil's serving of chicken-fried rice drew a gasp from Mary.

"You could feed an army with all that."

She herself settled for tea and soup and salad. Stewart's rivaled Phil's in quantity and consisted of a series of courses. Phil unwrapped his chopsticks and began to wield them with great dexterity.

"Or a navy," Phil said.

Their meals eaten and a fresh pot of hot tea called for, Stewart began to put to Mary the questions that needed answering.

"You were Fred's girl."

"His fiancée in all but name."

"What was the secret?"

"Naomi refused to accept the fact that he was breaking their engagement."

"She wouldn't give back the diamond ring?" Phil asked.

Mary smiled. "That wasn't the bone of contention."

"What was?"

"Her refusal to agree that everything between them was over."

They discussed this for some time. Phil remembered Naomi's flamboyant entrance at the funeral home, her place of prominence in Sacred Heart, occupying the front pew with the Nevilles, the near public quarrel with Mary in the university club that Roger had told him of.

"When did you last see him?"

Mary thought. "Sunday." The body had been found on Tuesday.

"Where was that?"

"We had dinner."

"Your mother says she knew nothing about you and Fred."

"She didn't. How I regret now that I didn't tell her. I think she imagines I dreamt the whole thing up."

"You last saw him on Sunday?"

"Yes."

"You didn't visit him at his apartment after that?"

"Certainly not."

"You never went to his apartment?"

Mary looked thoughtful. "He was very old-fashioned in many ways. It was one of the things that attracted me to him. He was careful to avoid anything that might affect my reputation."

Phil said, "That sounds like Fred. You know, he said nothing about you to Roger or me."

"Of course not. We were agreed that my mother would be told first when it could be made public."

"After Naomi capitulated?"

Mary nodded. "You can imagine what I thought of her, hanging on when there was no point, putting me in such an equivocal position. Oh, there were other reasons for not making a formal announcement." She looked at Phil. "You know how my mother was. She persisted in thinking of me as an old maid and was constantly trying to throw me at some man of her choice."

Stewart sipped his tea and said, "The manager of Fred's building said you visited Fred in his apartment between Sunday and the day his body was discovered."

Mary just shook her head. "No. I last saw him on Sunday."

"You're sure of that?"

"Of course I'm sure."

But she was not annoyed by the question. And so they had arrived at a dilemma. On the one hand, the building manager said Mary had been there during the days of Fred's absence without leave, on the other she said she had last seen Fred on the Sunday.

"He must be mistaken," Phil said. "The building manager."

"I don't know him and I don't see how he could have known me. He said I had been there?"

"Yes."

"That's odd."

And that was all. She did not protest at all, let alone too much. Phil could see that Stewart did not intend to press the matter. First he would want to talk again to the building manager.

They took Mary back to campus and then Stewart said, "I have to get a recent photograph of her. Asking her mother for one could be sticky."

Phil said, "No need to do that. We can stop at the apartment and pick up the university staff mug book. Mary should be in that."

And she was. Such photographs suggested driving license or passport photos, but were sufficient to serve their purposes.

"Where's Roger?" Jimmy Stewart asked.

Phil looked at his watch. "In class. This is his big day. Two classes."

"Wow."

Phil let it go. There was no need to explain the apparent easiness of the academic life. The scant time spent in classrooms would have been surprising if one did not know that professors are, in a sense, at it twenty-four hours a day. Actual teaching is the periodic dissemination of thoughts and materials that accumulate over the long haul, incubating, achieving organization. No doubt it was possible for a professor to prepare a few canned courses and grind them out year after year, leaving his time free for whatever else he chose to do. But that seemed to be rare to the point of non-existence, at least at Notre Dame.

Santander took some time to answer his door, but then the sound of the television made the door vibrate. Stewart pounded on it again and suddenly there was silence inside. Another minute and then the door opened and Santander looked out at them over a chain.

"IRS," Stewart said.

Santander gave a wary smile. "Come on."

"We need to talk."

"We already talked."

Stewart began to search the inner pocket of his suit jacket. "Well, if you insist on seeing the search warrant . . ."

"Just a minute."

The door closed, a chain rattled, Stewart avoided Phil's eyes, and soon they were inside.

"What were you watching?" Phil asked.

"Watching." Santander looked puzzled, then understood. "The box? I just keep it on for company."

Phil began to slap his knee with the staff mug book and Santander became curious.

"What's that?"

Stewart said, "You told me that Fred

120

Neville's girl visited him during the days he was missing."

"Missing? He was right there in his apartment all along."

"And you saw a girl visit him."

"Twice."

"Had you seen her before?"

"How else would I have recognized her?"

"Good point." Stewart asked Phil for the mug book. He opened it randomly and handed it to Santander. "You see her there?"

Santander brought the book to within inches of his nose and his head moved as typewriter carriages once had, from left to right, then return, another row, down one page and then the facing page. He looked over the book and shook his head. "No."

Stewart took the book from Santander and made as if to rise. Then, as if struck by a thought, opened the book, paged toward the back, and handed it again to Santander. Phil knew that Stewart had displayed the page on which Mary Shuster's photograph was prominent in the middle of a bottom row. They waited for Santander to reach the bottom of the page. He hesitated, then went on to the facing page. A slow reading of the rows of photographs there. He looked over the book, then closed it and handed it back to Stewart.

"Can't find her?"

"She's not there."

Stewart opened the book, stood beside Santander and pointed. "Is that her?"

Santander hardly glanced. "No. I told you she's not there."

"Okay." He looked at Phil. "No need to search the apartment, is there?"

Santander said, "I thought you already had."

"I meant yours."

A sputtering Santander accompanied them to the door. He stood in it until they were in Stewart's car and then closed it, audibly putting the chain back in place. In a moment they heard the roar of the television begin.

9 Members of the athletic department were housed in a suite of offices separate from those assigned the coaches of the major sports, and were, like those, located in the Joyce Convocation and Athletic Center. Fans entering the building for basketball or hockey games passed the doors of these suites unseeing. But then games were special occasions. The ordinary daily work of the department went on unwitnessed by the vast body of Irish fans, all but unknown to the faculty, except for those who still worked out in the Joyce Center. The building was irreverently called the geodesic bra, its pale twin domes lifting to the sky in saucy presentation. Across the street was the stadium, recently enlarged to accommodate eighty thousand fans, before which stood a magnificent bronze statue of Frank Leahy, the legendary wartime and postwar coach of the Fighting Irish. A bronze Moose Krause, the longtime athletic director, sat on a bench outside the center. The Joyce after whom the center was named was Father Ned Joyce, who had been vice president during the long presidency of Father Hesburgh. Father Joyce

was a gentle giant of a man who had retained his South Carolina accent and was credited with keeping the university financially afloat during the Hesburgh years as well as making sure that the athletic program was clean as a whistle.

The death of Fred Neville had cast its brief pall over the center and especially the sports information office where he had worked but, in the manner of such things, the pall lifted, the event began to recede into the past, work resumed. Only Anthony Boule seemed unable to shake off the dazed grief the death of Fred called for.

"I can't believe he's gone," he said to Thelma, the secretary.

"Yes." Thelma was long of tooth and thin of body, a paragon of efficiency and matter-of-factness.

"No one will ever really replace him."

"We'll just soldier on for now."

"I don't suppose there's been any talk of that?"

"Of what?"

"Fred's replacement."

Thelma looked at Anthony for a silent moment. "Are you going to apply?"

"Me!"

Anthony laid a stubby hand on where his heart was supposed to be. The unsuccessful beard was meant to compensate for his thinning hair. A favorite office sport had been for him and Fred to try to top one another with athletic lore, with the emphasis on Notre Dame. Anthony considered himself an expert on the postgraduation lives of Notre Dame athletes. Those who had gone on to professional careers were easy to track, but of course the vast majority of student athletes did not turn pro but continued in lines as various as the student body as a whole. Anthony had never been able to stump Fred, whose memory was a matter of wonderment to all. But then Fred had never stumped him in his favorite category — life after Notre Dame.

"Why not?"

"Has anyone mentioned it?"

Thelma tried her more alluring smile. "I just did."

"But you're prejudiced."

"In what way?"

He hesitated. Anthony did not have a long track record with women. The truth was that they frightened him, not least Thelma, whose interest carried the suggestion of some shared future. He had taken her to lunch half a dozen times; it was part of his daily ritual to take a chair beside her desk and shoot the bull. Until he realized that she did not consider herself just one of the guys and interpreted his attention in an alarming way. But in the days after the funeral, he had renewed the practice.

"You found Fred tough to work for."

"That's true. And of course Mary Shuster always took pride of place."

"How about her?" Anthony said.

"Her mourning? Apparently they were engaged."

"It wasn't apparent to his parents."

"But you saw them when she dropped by. If that was platonic I'm an Aristotelian."

Anthony let it go. Thelma knew things that he did not. He often felt stumped when speaking with her, not that she took on the triumphalist air Fred had when he got Anthony off his speciality and shamed him with the extent of his expertise. Anthony took pleasure in impressing others with his grasp of the history of Notre Dame sports, but in the privacy of his own heart he admitted that Fred had it all over him.

"Did Fred ever speak to you about Naomi McTear?" Thelma asked.

"Not in so many words."

She dipped her chin and looked at him

over her half glasses. "How then?"

"They always got together when Naomi was in town."

"But that was business."

"Sure it was. But a little monkey business too."

Thelma turned her chair toward him. "Tell."

"There's really nothing to tell."

"Come on."

He made her beg before he told her of what he had heard about the network apartment Naomi used when she was in town for Notre Dame games. One of the desk clerks there was a regular at Houlihan's, a sports bar a mile from the apartment. A bulbous fellow named Scott whose tone was insinuating and who believed that everyone but himself was living a bacchanalian life.

"You wouldn't believe what goes on there on game weekends."

They were sitting in Houlihan's, in the bar where a dozen television sets brought in every game in progress anywhere. Racing, one of several sports Anthony could not abide, was coming in on both sets in their immediate view.

"Parties?"

"You can call them that."

"Well, you have a good many footloose celebrities there."

Scott's brows danced significantly.

"Isn't that where the network crews put up?"

"A lot of them."

"Naomi McTear."

Scott reacted as if he had guessed the winning number. "I suppose you know about that since you work with him."

"Who?"

"Neville. Fred Neville."

How could he not be curious about what the man he considered his rival was up to. If anything. He waved away the suggestion.

"Fred and Naomi McTear."

That had been a year ago. Anthony continued to express disbelief, not giving Scott the satisfaction of thinking he believed him. But he did check it out and it was true. Back then it hadn't only been at the network apartment. Anthony had followed them one Saturday night to the Carriage House, where he waited for hours in his car, smoking surreptitiously, from time to time getting out to stretch his legs and stare at the night sky above with its sprinkling of stars. It was quiet as could be out there, though from time to time there was the distant sound of a plane taking off, one of the private craft flown in by the dozens by affluent fans. Anthony tried not to think of what he was doing, of what he would think of anyone else doing what he was doing. It was sneaky, it was low. He went back to his car and thought of leaving. Instead he lit a cigarette and continued to wait.

When finally they came out, it was clear they had supped and sipped well. In an elaborate display of joking gallantry, Fred opened the door for her and nearly fell backward as he did so. Clear tinkling laughter in the thin night air. Fred drove unsteadily out of the lot and headed back toward town. If he were stopped he would be in trouble. DUI. What a thing the local rag would make of that. Anthony, by contrast, felt as sober as a judge and it was with the eyes of a judge that he watched them emerge from the car at the building where Scott worked and go inside. So far nothing indictable. He had waited in vain. Still he decided to wait for Fred to come out and bring the whole silly evening to closure. But the minutes passed, and then a quarter hour, and Fred did not appear. Anthony, numb from lack of sleep and not welcoming the morning light, was still behind the wheel of his car when Fred appeared. It was nearly nine in the morning. He got into his car and drove off and Anthony went to his bed, pondering what he had witnessed.

It was a version of this, less unflattering to himself, that he told the toothy Thelma. No need to tell her that, while this had gone on for some months, it seemed to have stopped suddenly a few months ago. If Fred and Naomi were getting together it was not in the network apartment. His effort to strike up a friendship with Santander went nowhere.

"So he must have given her that rock."

Anthony shrugged.

"It's odd that we're surprised that celebrities can get as lonely as we do."

"Celebrities!"

"Naomi."

"Oh, sure." He had thought she meant Fred.

"It has to be a lonely life."

"Oh, I don't know. On the move, game preparation, friends from coast to coast."

"She wouldn't have had a Fred from coast to coast."

"How can you tell?"

"The diamond ring."

Anthony shrugged.

"Where are we having lunch?"

"I didn't know we were."

"That's why I told you."

What could he do? Thelma wouldn't be all that bad-looking if it weren't for her teeth. And they weren't that bad when she smiled. They went arm-in-arm into the snowy world.

IO "Mary wasn't the woman, Phil?"

"No. If there was such a woman. I would hate to have to rely on Santander's testimony in court. Besides, visiting someone is not a crime."

"Provided that someone was alive when one arrived and was not dead when one left."

"It must have been suicide, Roger."

"Must it?"

"Who has a motive? Mary loved the guy."

"Who was engaged to another woman."

"Which she knew because he told her. She understood that Naomi was not giving up easily."

Roger sat and hummed and then, as if despairing of achieving perfect pitch, said, "It is so hard to imagine Fred as the acute point of such a triangle. It was news enough when we learned about Mary, but suddenly there is Naomi. What a Bluebeard our friend has turned out to be."

"Bluebeard did the killing, Roger."

"You know what I mean."

"I know what you mean. What's for dinner?"

"Why don't we ask the Shusters over."

"To celebrate?"

"They needn't know the reason for it, but yes, to celebrate." Mary might not appreciate their relief at her innocence.

"Why don't we ask Griselda Novak too? She and I can talk sports."

"We'll ask Greg Whelan too."

It was a festive evening. Roger kept it simple — spaghetti, garlic bread, a huge bowl of salad, and Chianti for those who wanted wine, ice water for Roger, ever abstemious.

"You're such a Puritan, Roger," Marjorie Shuster said, her lips red with Chianti.

"Am I? The truth is, I don't tolerate alcohol well."

The real reason was that he did not like to muddle his mind, however convivial wine was. To the nondrinker, the effect of alcohol on others is far more obvious than it is to them. Voices rise, laughter comes more easily — but that, as both Belloc and Chesterton said, is the point of drinking. Roger could appreciate that, without the need to verify it in his own case. Besides, he was the principal host and wanted to be

133

on the qui vive for his guests. Griselda too had ice water with her meal, having decided between that and milk.

"I don't want to corrupt minors," Roger said.

"When I had dinner with Fred Neville, we shared a bottle of wine."

There was an uneasy silence, with Mary looking uncomfortable.

"God rest his soul," Roger said.

"Amen."

That difficult moment was soon behind them. Poor Phil had no luck in getting Griselda to talk about the upcoming Lady Irish home game the following night.

"Is it nationally televised?"

Griselda nodded. "Naomi McTear stayed on for this game. On assignment."

Another awkward moment.

Phil said, "When do the television crews arrive?"

"Oh, she comes days before. In order to prepare. That means she will have been here over a week."

"How so?" Roger asked.

"She came in on Friday for the Sunday game before Fred . . ." As if aware that her remarks caused Mary discomfort, Griselda let her voice drift away. She said to Roger, "Your class today was great."

"Now, now. You don't have to sing for your supper."

Griselda told the others, "He analyzed some sonnets of Maurice Francis Egan. They hadn't seemed much to me when I first read them."

"Those were poems Fred especially liked."

"He loved poetry."

Marjorie professed to be astounded. "Fred?"

"He wrote it too," said Phil.

Phil pushed back and clapped his head. "Good Lord, I forgot all about that."

The others stared at him. He rose and went off to his room. When he came back he held a folded sheet of paper.

"Jimmy Stewart and I found this in the fax machine in his apartment. Apparently he had sent it to himself from the office."

Mary asked to see it and began to read it, her lips moving.

"Read it aloud," Roger suggested. And she did.

Isadore of Seville loved etymology,
Loved to analyse the source of words,
Or invented them without apology,
Visigoths and others with their herds
Exchanged their tongues for Latin,
 more or less,

Mixing barbarian dialects with it.
Ancient authors always had the wit,
Received, then polished, with which they
  could express
Young thoughts in language old.
Soon the wine was watered,
  the language bastardized,
Harsh sounds, with meanings harsh with
  northern cold,
Upset the tongue that Virgil standardized.
Subject to invasion like the empire,
True Latin, having risen, fell.
Eventually in Seville our Isadore
Reverently misread the words in his
  provincial cell.

"Let me see it," Roger said, and Mary passed the poem to him.

"My Nathaniel wrote poetry," Marjorie said. "I must say it was far more intelligible than that."

"The poem is perfectly intelligible," said Mary.

"I'm with you, Marjorie," Phil said.

Griselda began again on Maurice Francis Egan's poetry but Roger was brooding over the page. His concentration silenced the others. He looked at Mary.

"You realize this is a love letter," he said to her.

"To whom?" Marjorie asked, and Mary just glanced at her mother.

"What do you mean, Roger?" Mary asked.

Roger handed the poem to her. "Read the first letters of the lines." Mary did so and as she did she fairly glowed. "For heaven's sake."

"Well, what is it?" Marjorie asked, and was echoed by Phil.

Mary handed the poem to her mother, who frowned over it for some minutes, then said, "I don't get it."

"Read the first letters of the lines. From top to bottom."

Marjorie did as she was instructed. "*I.L.O.V.E.M.A.R.Y.S.H.U.S.T.E.R.* Well!"

"That's beautiful," Griselda said.

"And it was written just days before he died. It is dated, you see."

"That is nice," Marjorie said, somewhat grudgingly. "Very nice."

"So you see, Mother, I was not making it up."

"Did I say you made it up?"

Griselda wanted to see the poem. She traced her finger down the page, silently pronouncing the opening letters. She then surrendered it to Mary. "You must keep it always."

But then Greg Whelan asked to see it. When he had read the poem for himself, he said to Mary, "I'll want a copy for the archives."

"That is a copy," Phil said. "The original is being held as possible evidence."

"Of what?"

"Oh, Mother."

Phil drove the Shusters and Griselda home, leaving Roger and Greg to talk. Greg had had his share of the wine and soon waxed sentimental.

"That poem certainly proves which of his two fiancées Fred loved."

"Only a man in love would use such an old trick."

"It must be hard to do."

"You and I will never know, Greg."

"Maybe, like Socrates, you will turn to writing poetry in your old age."

"Only if, like Socrates, I am condemned to death."

"How is the investigation into Neville's death going?"

"Why don't we wait for Phil before taking up that topic?"

When Phil returned he said, "Well, I broke down."

"The car?"

"No, no. I told the Shusters that Jimmy Stewart had been told Mary had visited Fred during the days he was missing but that this had been disproved."

Phil told Greg the story of Santander. "He said it was Fred's girl but when shown a photograph of Mary Shuster said she wasn't the woman."

"So who was?" Greg asked.

But all three of them were thinking the same thing, despite the profession of love that Fred had made in his last poem.

PART THREE

CAN YOU
FORGIVE
HER?

I Those personally concerned with a death said not to be due to natural causes must see it as the single most important event, the cynosure of every prurient eye, the topic of every whispering and doubtless malevolent lip. Of course this is not so, but the Nevilles, as the significance of what the police told them about their son's death sank in, knew a sadness deeper than grief. Had Fred destroyed himself? Detective Jimmy Stewart was noncommittal.

"Have you any reason to think he would have done that?"

"None." Mrs. Neville was the default speaker for the couple. "He loved his job, he loved being here at Notre Dame."

"And he was engaged to Naomi McTear."

Mrs. Neville looked away. "Yes."

"So you must know her rather well."

"Oh, not at all. Once she came by our place in Phoenix, when she was passing through, to introduce herself and tell us about her and Fred."

"Is that how you learned of the engagement?"

"This was shortly afterward, apparently."

"Those are lovely rings," Stewart said.

Mrs. Neville held out her hands as if for inspection.

"What is that diamond?"

"My engagement ring." She cast a loving glance at her husband, who seemed mildly sedated.

"But I thought Fred gave your engagement ring to Naomi."

"My engagement ring? Certainly not. My rings will go with me to the grave."

"Hmmm."

"Why would you think such a thing?"

"I must have misunderstood."

"Is that what she said?" Mr. Neville asked.

"As I say, I must have misunderstood."

"Surely Fred couldn't have told her that."

Stewart asked if they would like to go through their son's apartment.

"I thought it was sealed off."

"I can let you in."

But Mr. Neville shook his head. "Not yet."

"How long will you be staying?"

"Until we know what happened to Fred."

It is always cruel when parents lose a child, but when the parents are elderly and the child an adult, it is in its way more difficult rather than less. The Nevilles were clearly in the last act of their lives, knew that and accepted it, and could not have dreamt that Fred would die before them. Suicide seemed more and more unlikely, and Stewart wished he could assure the Nevilles that it was impossible that their son had taken his own life. He hoped to be able to give them that assurance today. Roger Knight had asked the obvious question.

"Did you find the poison in the apartment?"

"Only in the cup from which he had been drinking."

Stewart had arranged to meet the Knights at Fred's apartment after this call on the Nevilles. He was allowed to continue working on Fred Neville's death only because of the department's concern to keep the matter as much under wraps as possible. The fact that Phil was working with him, courtesy of the university, justified assigning only Stewart to the case, and that lessened the drain on departmental resources. Even so, the media people, who had lavishly covered the funeral, largely because of the presence of coaches and players, and then subsided, had now, in the person of Laura Reith, shown renewed interest.

"What's up?" she had asked, sailing into Stewart's office in battle dress. She affected denims, men's shirts, and what might have been combat boots. Emerging from this proletarian apparel that all but concealed her gender was the loveliest face seen around police headquarters. Auburn hair, a complexion of natural tan, and pouty lips that seemed perpetually pursed to be kissed.

"I am," Stewart said, rising from his chair.

Laura sat in a chair and threw her denimed legs out before him, making an easy exit difficult.

"Why are you still following up on the Neville death?"

"Routine."

"Sure. You and Philip Knight are just staving off boredom. Was it suicide?"

"No, he gagged while reading the local paper."

Laura laughed. She was a reporter for the local television station that was a rival of the one owned by the local paper.

"I want an interview with Naomi McTear. Has she left town?"

146

"Some people work for a living."

"Well, I'm going to follow up on it. Nice story. Notre Dame sports information person, cable television sideline commentator. Sounds like conflict of interest. She seemed even prettier in person."

"Did she?"

Had Laura any inkling what a knockout she herself was? Stewart was certain she did. The way she dressed was meant to neutralize that but until and unless she wore a mask no one could fail to be struck by her.

"Oh, come on."

"The prettiest girls go into journalism nowadays."

Laura thought about it, as if the remark did not concern herself. She nodded. "If not pretty then pert and perky."

"Hannah Storm."

"Who's the one who does tennis?"

Laura looked at him with narrowed eyes. "You're dodging me, aren't you?"

"In what sense?"

"Ho, ho. Did Fred Neville commit suicide?"

"It's possible."

"So is a smart detective. Is it plausible?"

"Ask a smart detective."

"I just did."

"I don't think so. In an hour, I'll know for pretty sure."

"It's still an open question?"

"What's a closed question?"

"What it sounds like. What will decide the matter?"

If he went on talking to Laura like this he would be late to let the Knights into Fred's apartment. "Look, I'll get back to you."

"Or vice versa."

2   Scott Frye regarded his employment at Hoosier Residences as a disguise and took some pleasure in playing the role of obsequious menial behind the lobby desk, deferential to the residents, taking secret pleasure in the thought that they took him at face value. How could they guess that his head was filled with scenarios of the screenplays he intended to write? Nathanael West had been a room clerk. Mike Nichols had gone into almost monastic seclusion after he and Elaine May stopped making their hilarious dialogues, tapes of which Scott had all but memorized. After years of hibernation during which he seemed to have spent most of his time in bed, alone, Nichols emerged as the director of *Who's Afraid of Virginia Woolf?* And the rest was history. So too Scott thought of himself as germinating at HR, awaiting the spring when he would awake from his apparent slumber and be revealed as his true self. Meanwhile he had to deal with the invariably bitchy Naomi McTear. He had made the mistake of expressing his condolences when she passed his desk on her way out.

"Do I know you?"

"Only in my official capacity."

"Do you know me?"

"Ditto."

Q.E.D. apparently. Scott retained his fixed professional smile after having been put so decisively in his place. Could her manner be due to profound grief? He doubted it, he knew not why. For all her daring decolletage, the milk of human kindness was not a phrase that leapt to mind in dealing with Naomi McTear. The staff called her McTerror.

The cable network owned four suites in the building and Naomi was a frequent presence, more so during the past year, and the reason was Fred Neville. He had spent the night with her a couple times but in recent months the couple had seemingly decided on being more discreet and Fred was seldom seen on the premises. When Scott had told Anthony about this early on he invited the impression that assignations at HR were an established thing with the couple. Anthony had been eager to hear more and how could a future world-renowned screenwriter fail to provide a prurient story line? Anthony had eaten it up.

"What he like?" Scott asked. "I mean at work."

"Fred? He's good."

"He your boss?"

"Don't be ridiculous."

Aha. So he had fed Anthony a few more imaginary bones to gnaw on.

Scott went out back for a smoke and while he was shivering and trying to pretend he was enjoying his cigarette the door opened and one of the cleaning ladies came outside dragging two large plastic bags. This was one of the youngsters who still thought of her employment as glamorous. Scott stepped forward, glanced at her name tag, and said, "I'll take those, Heather."

"Oh, thank you." She in turn glanced at his name tag. "Mr. Scott." A bit of a downer that, but then the cleaning ladies did not frequent the front desk.

"Where is this stuff from?"

"It's on the bags."

And so it was, the number of the suite stenciled onto the plastic bags. Scott hadn't known of this practice. But then a desk clerk did not frequent the office of resident maintenance. Heather was shivering. "Go on inside, I'll take care of these."

Scott took the bags toward the Dumpster at the back of the parking lot, hearing

151

the door close behind him, indicating that Heather had gone inside. The sack in his right hand bore the number of the suite that had been used by Naomi McTear. Scott propped it against the back bumper of his car and took the other to the Dumpster and threw it in. On the way back, he popped his trunk, and dumped the other sack inside. By such random and irrational deeds the course of history is altered. In words somewhat to that effect, Scott returned to his desk.

It had been an impulsive deed, one done without forethought or plan, just done. He gave as little thought to it afterward as before, and so it was that for some days the black plastic sack of detritus from the suite of Naomi McTear lay forgotten in the trunk of Scott Frye's car.

3　Mary Shuster carried with her the poem in which Fred Neville had, in coded form, declared his love for her, carried it as Pascal had carried his Memorial sewn into the lining of his coat, as Descartes had carried with him the account of the dreams on the basis of which he had given philosophy a new and fateful turn. The poem itself made little sense to her and she could believe that Fred had written it only to convey the message of the opening letters of its lines.

The trauma of Fred's death, the wake and funeral, the awful news that he had died of poisoning, were slowly giving way to emptiness. She had never felt so lonely in her life. The telephone on her desk rang but it was never Fred on the line. There would never again be a call from Fred. And when the afternoon lengthened and lights were turned on against the winter dusk the time came when she would have gone off to see Fred at the Joyce Center.

Snow was falling softly when she emerged from the building, drifting dreamily in the soft glow of the lamps along the campus walkways. Mary set off across the campus, walking with her head back to allow the snowflakes to moisten her face. Her tears merged with the melted snow. She went through a little quadrant of residence halls and then around the great bulk of the library, proceeding on a diagonal, past O'Shaughnessy into the main mall and continuing to the law school. She crossed the oval and went along the walk that passed the Morris Inn and Alumni Center. The parking lot in front of the bookstore was, as always, full, the cars losing their shapes under the accumulation of snow. And then she was passing Cedar Grove Cemetery. She stopped, looked ahead and then behind, and then permitted herself to weep convulsively as she had not yet done, lamenting her lost future.

When she turned onto Angela Boulevard toward home, she wondered if it had been wise to agree with Fred that they must wait to announce their engagement until he had straightened out things with Naomi Mc-Tear. Mary was not a great sports fan, as this is reckoned at Notre Dame, but she had seen and not especially liked Naomi when she appeared breathless on the screen from the sidelines of a game. Her dislike of the woman had grown and, after the events of recent days, had almost settled into unchristian hatred.

"Naomi McTear!" she had said when Fred first told her of his involvement with the television reporter.

"I find it hard to believe myself."

"Was your engagement announced?"

"It's hard to explain."

"Is it?"

"Mary, I feel trapped. It sounds ridiculous, but things just happened and before I knew it she was talking of getting married."

"*She* was?"

"I said it sounds ridiculous."

"Well, it certainly does. Did you formally propose to her?"

He fell into an embarrassed silence and Mary found that she did not want to press him on the matter. She did not want to find out what form his relationship with Naomi had taken. Fred was always so respectful of her, almost too much so, but she sensed a nobility in it.

"You gave her your mother's ring."

"No, I didn't."

"Fred, I saw it. Everyone did. She made sure of that."

"That is *her* mother's ring."

"Hers! How could you give her her own mother's ring?"

"I didn't. Oh my God, this is hard to explain.

Now Mary wanted to know. "Tell me," she said gently.

It had not been enjoyable to hear but it was obviously more agonizing for Fred to tell. At first, it was simply in the line of duty. It was his job to supply reporters with the information they needed to be as knowledgeable as possible about the players, the coaches, various statistics, past and present. Naomi was a reporter, often the only female reporter, and she demanded and got special attention. Fred told her of the dinner at the Carriage House and its aftermath, more by suggestion than directly, but Mary got the picture.

"She lured you to her room."

"I was a free agent."

"You said you feel trapped and I can understand that. You are. You were. Fred, break it off. She has no legitimate hold on you. I assume you do want to break it off."

"Oh, Mary."

She let him take her in his arms, unconsciously recognizing the vulnerability of the contrite male. Men are such fools in matters of love, meaning sex. But then so are women. Anthony unmanned himself for Cleopatra, but she ended with an adder on her bosom. Literature is largely the record of the follies of men and women, ruled by their passions, heedless of consequences, and later wracked by remorse. Naomi's edge had been the disarming brazenness with which she had pursued her quarry. Of course Fred had been helpless before such an onslaught. Any man would have been. Well, most men.

"Can you forgive me?"

"First you must forgive yourself. I hope you've been to confession about this."

She felt him grow uneasy. Confessions were heard daily on campus, in Sacred Heart, elsewhere. It was Mary's practice once a month to slip over to the basilica at 11:15 when confessions were heard before the 11:30 Mass. One of the perks of working at Notre Dame was that absence for devotion was never questioned. An annoying thing about those midday confessions were the troops of tourists being led around by officious guides, speaking in loud tones. Bald or silver-haired or both, their blazers a kind of uniform, these guides were retired laymen who found in the mild authority of leading a tour a sufficient last hurrah. The confessionals were an object of interest. Tourists would lag behind and sometimes open a confessional door and peek in, expecting who knew what Maria Monk disporting. Once, while confessing, Mary had heard the door open and then quickly close. Dear God. It was bad enough to whisper her sins through the grille to the priest but the thought of being an object on display for tourists distracted her.

"I didn't hear that, Father."

The priest had been in full flight when she said this. He was young, zealous, and had obviously prepared a set piece for penitents that day. Her interruption threw him off. There was a moment of silence.

"I will give you absolution now."

"And my penance?"

Another silence. "Are you staying for Mass?"

"Yes, Father."

"Offer it up for the poor souls in purgatory."

And he went into the long form of the formula of absolution, speaking rapidly. Mary had strained to follow him; she wanted to hear every word of it.

After his revelation about Naomi, Mary advised Fred to avail himself of that midday opportunity to get his slate clean. He stepped back and looked at her. Then drew her to him again and kissed her passionately.

"God bless you, Mary."

Walking home with snow falling like a benediction on the world she prayed for the repose of Fred's soul. The thought of dedicating her life to her lost love had occurred to her when she decided to attend the wake and funeral all in black. His death had made her a widow of sorts. The future with him she had dreamt of would never be, but in some ways they were closer now, as if she could communicate with him in the privacy of her mind. The thought of sacrificing herself to his memory had a powerful attraction. It would be an acceptable equivalent of Dido throwing herself on the burning pyre so the escaping Aeneas could see how powerfully her love for him had affected her. Not a very close analogy, but Mary understood what she meant.

When she got home, she came in the kitchen door, stamped snow from her feet, hung up her coat and went into the living room to find Anthony Boule sitting cozily with her mother before the fire.

4   The first thing that Anthony had thought when Scott Frye told him of Fred Neville and Naomi McTear's liaison was, "Poor Mary." When she would come to the Joyce Center to see Fred at the end of a day, Anthony was all but invisible to her. She had eyes for Fred alone. When he was noticed, doubtless as a result of some joking remark of Fred's, Mary had glanced at Anthony but little more. But if he was invisible to her, she was an object of enormous interest to him, all the more so after Anthony heard of Fred's shenanigans with Naomi. Odd that he never envied Fred the attention the flashy television celebrity lavished on him. Naomi at least noticed him, but then she was aware of every male presence. It was that which had prevented Anthony from suspecting anything between her and Fred; her manner toward him was one of impersonal affection, generic, or so Anthony had thought. Who would have suspected Fred Neville of being a Romeo?

Fred's role in Anthony's fantasies was as the man who had usurped the role meant for him. Anthony was not a Domer — his degree was from Boston College — but like most Catholics, he gave Notre Dame his primary allegiance. He had first come to campus as student manager of a BC team, had marveled at the offices of the sports information director, the efficiency with which things were done, the easy affluence of the place. From that first visit he felt he had found his destiny.

He took every occasion to establish a bond with the office, he haunted the place on BC visits, and the summer before his senior year he was taken on as a student intern. The following spring, the position Fred Neville eventually obtained had been announced and Anthony immediately threw his hat into the ring. At his own expense he had made several trips to South Bend. He was certain his claim on the position was strong. That he had not been wholly deluded became clear after the job went to Fred. Anthony received a call saying a lesser job had fallen open and was he interested. He accepted even before he got the job description.

It turned out that his status was little more than that he'd had as student intern, the main difference being that it was year-round and paid more than Anthony would having imagined. After he graduated, he moved to South Bend and began the long agony of living in the shadow of Fred Neville. Thelma alone had noticed how difficult this was for him, and hers was not a sympathy he craved.

"I was sure you'd get the job," she said over beer in the back bar of the university club a week after Anthony's arrival.

"I'm thankful for what I have."

"Oh, come on."

"It may be the bottom rung but at least I'm on the ladder."

She thought about that. "A healthy attitude," she decided.

He was not at all that philosophical about it, but he did not want her pity.

In humble moments, he could admit Fred was superior to him. He had journalistic experience between graduation and being taken on at the sports information department, he was a graduate of Notre Dame, he was an encyclopedia. When he referred to Fred as Google only Thelma understood. She laughed a toothy laugh.

"That's your great advantage. You have a sense of humor."

Did he? He found it hard to laugh when Mary was in Fred's office. Thelma seemed to be his consolation prize, but he found little consolation. Still, it was nice to have a sympathetic ear and someone who voiced the sentiments he was too proud to state himself. It came down to the fact that he was jealous of Fred and from this it followed, as night the day, that he must yearn for Mary Shuster's attention.

"If she only knew," Thelma said, after Anthony had passed on Scott's revelation.

"Of course I couldn't even hint." Was this a hint that Thelma might?

But if he was invisible to Mary, Thelma was even more so, giving her a resentment of her own.

"The professor's daughter. There are families like that here. They consider themselves to be still basking in a lost prominence."

"Her father is on the faculty?"

"Was. He died at least a decade ago."

Fred's friendship with the Knights seemed to firm up his link with Mary Shuster and her mother. Anthony's efforts to get in with the Knights had not been wholly successful. Roger was out of reach, Anthony had attended an evening lecture by the huge Huneker Professor of Catholic Studies and it had all been Greek to him. But Philip Knight sometimes came by the office and Anthony had secured an introduction from Fred.

"This guy knows it all," Fred had said.
"What's all?"

"Ask him a question. About sports."

Phil thought a bit, then said, "Frank Leahy."

He had hit on Anthony's absolutely strongest suit. Leahy had coached at Boston College before coming to Notre Dame. Anthony sometimes thought of himself as the sports-information equivalent of the legendary Leahy. He emptied his mental file on Leahy and Phil Knight had been impressed. He said to Fred, "No wonder you speak so highly of him."

Was this true? Anthony was abashed. Fred had never praised him to his face but it was particularly sweet to hear that he was praised in his absence.

"Fred is the memory man around here," he said generously.

But it had never really got beyond that. Even so, it was a whole lot better than his invisibility to Mary.

Mary worked in the registrar's office and Anthony made a point of having lunch in Grace Hall on an average of once a week, in the hope that he would run into her. But all he got was a vague nod in return to his greeting. Besides, she was always with somebody, too often with Fred Neville.

The rock Naomi had flashed at the wake and funeral had never been on display in her visits to the Joyce Center, Thelma assured Anthony.

"I would have noticed, Antoine. How could you not notice anything about such a classy dresser. I suppose like all the other men your eyes are on her legs."

Like Naomi, Thelma wore skirts of minimal length, but there was no gasping when she crossed her legs in imitation of Naomi and lifted her toothy smile to visitors. Mary, by contrast, favored ankle-length skirts or pantsuits. But it was not because she had skinny pins like Thelma.

Anthony had driven past the Shuster home in Harter Heights, he had plotted and planned on ways to run into her by accident. But his imagination failed him. When Fred's body was found, his first impulse had been to want to talk to her, but it was not until the wake that he had been able to confront her, all in black.

"What an awful thing," he said.

Mary nodded, accepting her role as chief mourner. Anthony did not begrudge her this. Fred's death had put her on the open market and although this was not the time to act on that, he had gained something when he fell into conversation with Mary's

165

mother, Marjorie Shuster.

"I was just speaking to Mary."

Mrs. Shuster's reaction was puzzling.

"They made a wonderful couple."

"I knew nothing about it," Mrs. Shuster said.

"We all did at the Joyce Center."

"You work there?"

"Why don't we sit down."

They sat and Mrs. Shuster talked about the good old days and Anthony was glad to listen. The following day in the university club he again sought out Mrs. Shuster and was treated to another disquisition on Notre Dame, and her husband, Nathaniel. Nathaniel proved to be the open sesame. The widow was delighted by his interest, and began to speak of her late husband's library.

"I'd love to see it."

"Just stop by when you have time and I'll show it to you."

And so it was that he stopped by and was ensconced with Marjorie Shuster by the fire when Mary came in.

5 The hard drive of the computer in Fred Neville's office made it clear that the poem Phil had found in the tray of the fax machine and copied had not been a onetime effort. The file called *Egan* contained several dozen poems, half of them unfinished. One of the few finished ones was the declaration of Fred's love for Mary Shuster via thoughts on Isadore of Seville.

Roger and Greg Whelan had been let into the apartment by Stewart, who had to wake up the aged cop on duty in a chair beside the taped door. When Roger and Greg got settled at the computer, Jimmy left them to their work.

By and large, Roger and Greg took turns examining the files on Fred's computer, working in silence, both feeling somewhat sheepish about looking through their dead friend's work. Perhaps they both feared coming upon something, well, surprising. After all, Roger thought, Fred had proved himself to be something of an enigma. Not in his manner, not in what he had said or done, but in the large dimensions of his life that he had chosen to keep hidden.

First, there had been Mary Shuster, surprise enough. Not that she wasn't a wonderful girl. Roger liked her almost as much as he did her mother. Marjorie was a living link to the Notre Dame of yesteryear, her memories evoking an all but lost world. Doubtless it takes eyes to see such things, but neither Roger nor Phil had had any inkling of Fred's devotion to her. Second, more than a surprise, was Naomi McTear. Phil had known who she was, her public persona, as it were, he had seen her on television, but to Roger she had been less than a name and when he had seen her at Fred's wake and funeral and later at the university club he did not face the difficulties of those for whom a person is at once a stranger and as familiar as a friend. In any case, it had been to Roger rather than to Phil that Naomi had chosen to come.

Roger was alone in the apartment when the phone had rung.

"Professor Knight, please?"

"This is Roger Knight."

"Naomi McTear. I'm on my way to the airport and wonder if I could see you before I leave."

"Where are you calling from?"

"I'm in a rental car, approaching the campus."

Roger gave her directions to the Notre Dame Village and, after he hung up, pondered the reason for this unexpected visit. He knew this woman only from her somewhat dramatic appearance at Fred Neville's wake and subsequent appearance at the funeral and the university club, the last one in which an open quarrel between her and Mary Shuster had been narrowly averted. Phil spoke highly of her in her professional role and this estimate had not been affected by what Phil had witnessed at the funeral home. In any contest between Naomi McTear and Mary Shuster, Roger knew which woman he himself would champion, but what contest could there be now with Fred no longer among the living?

The young woman who came to his door ten minutes later bore little resemblance to the fashionable young woman he had hitherto seen. She was dressed for travel, informal, comfortable in jeans, a turtleneck sweater, and a large olive-colored jacket that hung loosely from her shoulders. She wore a baseball cap with the letters of her TV channel prominent above the bill.

"Thanks for seeing me."

"You say you're on your way to the airport?"

She shook a sleeve and a large mannish watch appeared on her left wrist. The absence of the diamond ring was in striking contrast to the way she had flouted it at the wake and funeral. "I should be at the airport in an hour."

"There's coffee on."

"Oh, good."

When they were settled with mugs of coffee, she sipped and smiled at Roger. "I can't have made a good impression on you at the university club the other day."

"It was a trying occasion."

"I am still trying to convince myself that this has happened."

"You have lost a fiancé."

"Do I detect a skeptical tone?"

"Do I detect an absence of diamond ring?"

"I never wear it when I'm traveling. Too flashy."

"You and Fred were engaged?"

"He wanted out," she said simply. "He said there was someone else."

"Mary Shuster?"

"Yes."

"Well, all that is moot now."

"I had refused to let him break our engagement."

"You needn't tell me this."

"I know. Did Fred ever mention me to you?"

"No."

"And you were a good friend. I know that. He spoke of you to me."

"The fact is, I had no idea there was anything between Fred and Mary. Sometimes I think I miss all the obvious things."

She looked at him through half-closed eyes. "But not the important things?"

"Being caught between two women can hardly be called unimportant."

"Not to the two women anyway. I had no idea it would drive Fred to do anything so desperate."

"What do you mean?"

She drank some coffee, then spoke into the mug in a whisper. "Suicide."

"Do you think that's what it was?"

She looked surprised. "Don't you?"

"It's possible, of course. Logically possible. But knowing Fred as I did I find it hard to believe."

"I feel the same way."

"When did you see him last?"

She thought about it. "Friday. I came in on Friday to cover the Saturday game. I was there when he briefed the media."

"On Saturday?"

She nodded.

"He didn't come to his office on Monday. His body was discovered on late Tuesday. Where do you stay when you're in town?"

She shifted her weight. "Why do you ask that?"

"Just curious."

"Is that all?"

"What else could there be?"

Silence. And then, "Nothing. I saw him on Sunday too. That was the last time."

"Ah."

"Not where I stay. Not at his apartment. We had a late breakfast at the Morris Inn."

"And that was the last time?"

"Yes."

"And you returned when you heard that he was dead?"

A little gasp. "I still can't get used to that."

"You said you wanted to talk."

"And we are. I wanted to make a better impression on you than I had in the university club."

Roger sensed that there was something she wanted to learn from him rather than something she had come to tell him. He asked her about her job and she dismissed the question. "None of that seems important now."

"Where are you off to?"

"Chicago. I have a brother there who hates Notre Dame."

"Poor fellow."

She laughed. "That's the sort of thing he hates."

She stayed for forty-five minutes, then rose to go. At the door, she turned and kissed Roger on the cheek, then hurried out to her car. He watched her get in, start the motor, wave, and drive off. Strange woman.

Roger pondered the significance of her visit but did not mention it to Phil. His thoughts turned to Fred's apartment. When he and Greg had examined the computer there they had agreed there was nothing on the hard drive relevant to Fred's death. As they left, the policeman on guard tried the door of the apartment to make sure it was locked, and then restored the yellow tape before sinking with a sigh into his chair. He smiled, and said, "Tough duty."

He indicated the bug in his ear and the wire that led to the radio in his pocket. "Rush Limbaugh."

The day after Naomi's surprise visit, Roger returned with Greg to Fred's address. He knocked on the building manager's door and had to knock twice more before a man looked out angrily over the security chain.

"Mr. Santander?"

"Who are you?"

"A detective."

The manager stared at Roger and then laughed.

"You have met my partner. He was here with Jimmy Stewart."

"So?"

"Could we come in for a minute?"

"Who's he? Another brother?"

"Ah, you noticed the resemblance."

"Just a minute?"

"If that."

The door closed, the chain was unhooked and the door opened.

"No need even to sit, Mr. Santander." Roger fumbled in the large pockets of his hooded jacket. He found what he wanted and handed it to Santander.

"Is she the one?"

"That's her!"

"Well, thank you. That's all."

"But what's it mean?"

"We're still working on it."

Santander was as reluctant to let them go as he had been to let them in. He stood in his open door and Greg assisted Roger to the car.

"Brother," he mumbled.

"In a large sense of the term. All men are brothers."

"What did you show him?"

"A photograph of Naomi McTear."

6   "I hope you remember me, Professor Knight."

"Ah, yes," Roger said. The fellow who had come half on the run to greet him when he entered the sports information office looked familiar.

"Anthony Boule." The smile was replaced by a mournful expression. "I was a friend of Fred Neville."

"Of course. You can show me his office. I have been asked to check his computer for any light it might shed on recent events."

"The police asked us to keep it locked."

"I am here at the behest of the police."

A woman behind Anthony spoke. "Lieutenant Jimmy Stewart called to tell me you were coming."

Anthony stepped aside and a lanky young woman stood and thrust out her hand. "Thelma Maynooth. I have the key."

The two of them convoyed Roger to a door and Thelma unlocked it.

Anthony said, "I thought the police took the key."

"This is a master key."

"Some security."

"Anthony, I could hardly turn over the

176

master key to them. What if someone lost his key?"

"Who locks their door anyway?"

She ignored him. Her smile seemed to reveal more than the usual number of teeth. Something glittered at the side of her nose. It seemed to be a sequin. She turned and unlocked the door.

"If there's anything you need?"

"Thank you."

Roger went into Fred's office with Anthony following. He called out, "Thelma, bring us coffee, will you?"

"Have you broken a leg?"

"Great kidder," Anthony said. "What are you looking for?"

"I don't know."

Anthony took the great hooded coat with Notre Dame Swimming lettered across its expansive back. It was something Phil had picked up for Roger, courtesy of Fred. It had seemed to have a new significance when he told Griselda of floating across the pool in naval boot camp. Anthony hung the jacket on a coat tree and pulled out the chair behind the desk. He looked at it and then at Roger.

"I'll see if I can find something more comfortable."

"That will do."

Roger lowered himself tentatively into Fred's chair, squeezing his bottom between its arms. "I may need help getting out of this."

Anthony laughed, but it was not a skeptical laugh.

Roger swung the chair to the right and rolled up to the computer and turned it on. Thelma appeared with a cup of coffee and put it on the desk.

"Thanks a lot," Anthony said.

"I am sure Professor Knight would prefer to do what he has to do alone."

Good girl. She took Anthony's arm and led him from the office, pulling the door shut as they left.

It has been thought that graphology would go the way of other outmoded arts — plastering, bookbinding, calligraphy — with the advent of the computer. But then it had been thought that paper would become obsolete too and far more paper was consumed in the age of the computer than in the age of the typewriter. The typewriter had proved to be a personalized tool, at least when used by someone like Ezra Pound. His typewritten letters had been utterly distinctive, but then he had spelled words whimsically too. Each user of a computer tends to use it in his own way, if only in the naming of files. A feature of Fred's use was his eschewal of capitals and all punctuation other than dots in his e-mail messages. Roger began by scanning the files on the hard drive. *Egan* was there, doubtless the duplicate of the file he and Greg had found on the computer in Fred's apartment. A file named *ad meipsum* caught Roger's eye, and he called it up on the screen.

It was a diary of sorts, written in the manner of Fred's e-mail messages, block paragraphs preceded by a date. *12.x.02* marked the first entry, so the file had only recently been begun.

Call her not naomi that is beautiful
but mara that is bitter . . . mary has
far more cause for bitterness and she
is wonderfully understanding far more
than I deserve . . . in 19th century
novels like ralph the heir a man cd
get engaged inadvertently, trapped by
a heedless remark but this is the third
millennium and a moments weakness
should not carry a life sentence . . .
post coitum triste indeed . . . she has
taken to wearing a ring of her
mothers and calling it her engagement
ring . . . what I lack is ruthlessness . . .

I cannot even get angry with her . . . I too feel that my fall has obligated me and she senses that and that is her leverage . . . dear God I cannot explain it to Mary, only hint, which is bad enough . . . the thought of asking tom to intervene comes and goes but I know that wd do it . . . he hates nd and consequently me and wd likely do anything to prevent his sister from being permanently connected with nd

Roger pushed away from the computer and picked up the coffee he had been given by Thelma. As he brought it to his lips, he stopped, thinking of the cup that had been found on Fred's bedside table. But he sipped it with relish and put it on the desk, remembering Santander's identification of Naomi as the woman who had visited Fred's apartment during the days he had stayed away from this office.

"He was sure?" Phil asked.

"He didn't hesitate."

"I have to let Jimmy Stewart know."

"Of course. But I wanted to tell you first."

"What led you to show Santander Naomi's photograph?"

"A hunch."

"Thank God you had it. It may mean

nothing, but it definitely takes Mary off the hook."

Stewart came immediately to the apartment to hear the story of the identification from Roger himself. Then he fell silent.

"So what does it mean?"

"She falls into the category of the woman scorned."

And Roger developed the thoughts that had been forming in his mind since leaving Santander. By Naomi's own admission, she had been holding Fred to an engagement that was at best equivocal. That had been one of the reasons for his and Mary's secrecy about their informal but far less equivocal engagement.

"He wanted to dump her?"

"He hadn't even proposed to her."

"But the ring she was flashing for all to see?"

"She put it on her own hand. It belonged to her mother."

Phil shook his head at the wiles of the woman.

Stewart said, "She left town?"

"She was on her way to the airport when she stopped to talk."

"Roger, why didn't you tell me this yesterday?"

"One, it probably doesn't mean anything. Two, I thought of the effect on Mary if it became known that Naomi had visited him in his apartment."

"She wasn't staying there, was she?" Stewart asked.

"No." Roger paused. This had not occurred to him. "Her network owns several apartments in Hoosier Residences. She was coming from there when she stopped to see me."

"You should have told me at once," Stewart said.

"He's right, Roger."

"Of course, he is."

"You said she was on her way to Chicago? To catch another plane?"

"She mentioned Chicago as her destination. I suppose you could check that."

Stewart said grimly, "I am going to check a number of things."

"I'll come with you," Phil said."

So it had been a somewhat crestfallen Roger who had set off for the Joyce Center in his golf cart, maneuvering along the snowy campus walks. His only consolation was that in talking to Naomi his worst suspicions had dissolved. She had been forthright, telling him far more than she had to. She needn't have told him anything at all. But now, with Fred's *ad meipsum* file on the screen before him, he could imagine that her visit had been intended to allay any suspicions he might have had. She had provided him with what would have been her motive, a woman scorned. He remembered the expression on Phil's face. Naomi might very well be a wily woman indeed.

He scanned through other entries in the file and came to the last, dated the Thursday before the game Naomi was in town to cover.

It was a mistake to run up to chicago to see tom . . . I took the south shore and that is always a treat, having called beforehand to see if tom was there . . . we agreed to meet at a German restaurant . . . we ordered a schooner of beer and his manner did not make it easy to bring up naomi . . . i said something banal about how nice that a brother and sister had both ended up in sports . . . not as players, he said, and that seemed the end of that topic . . . he brought up what I had come to talk about . . . are you and naomi seeing one another . . . well, we had dinner with you . . . I sensed something . . . I shrugged,

wondering what next . . . leave her
alone, neville . . . I mean that . . .
she has a great career but it wd be
over if she were connected to
nd . . . you know what I mean . . .
tell me . . . how serious are you
about her . . . I told him I was in
love with another woman . . . that
seemed to provide him momentary
relief, but then he asked, does
naomi know . . . then I tried to
explain to him the dilemma I was in
and he did not like the description
of his sister as someone chasing
after a guy who was anxious to drop
her . . . she thinks we're engaged, I
said . . . thinks . . . I never
proposed . . . she started wearing
her mother's ring and calling it our
engagement ring . . . he had noticed
her wearing that but had recognized
it as his mother's and didn't see any
further significance in it . . . he
wanted to know if I had told naomi
of the other woman . . . I've begged
her to forget me . . . we hadn't
ordered any food but he waved for
more beer . . . he was steaming . . .
when it came he chugalugged a
glass and then leaned toward

me . . . I don't believe a goddam word you've said . . . why did you come to me with this cock and bull story . . . so I told him . . . I hoped you wd talk to her . . . he sat back and glared at me . . . you are one arrogant sonofabitch, do you know that? Will you talk to her? He leaned forward again . . . I will talk to you . . . leave my sister alone . . . I don't know what your game is but I never heard such a story in my life . . . promise me you will leave her alone . . . by then I was mad too . . . promise me you'll tell her to leave me alone . . . that's when he dashed what beer was left in his glass in my face and got to his feet. This is your treat, neville . . . you can pay the bill . . . he left and I wiped his beer off my face . . . in a way it was a successful trip . . . I am sure he will talk to naomi

Roger finished his coffee. The scene Fred described was vividly before him. He wished he had found this file before taking to Stewart. Here was something more for him to check out.

The door opened and Anthony looked in.

185

"Everything going all right?"

"Come in."

"You sure?"

"Sit down."

Anthony shut the door and sat across from Roger, bright-eyed and receptive.

"You knew Fred pretty well, I suppose."

"We were colleagues."

"What was there between him and Naomi McTear?"

"Naomi! He was going out with Mary Shuster." Anthony added quickly, "I don't know how serious it was."

"But you knew both young women."

The corners of Anthony's mouth went down and his shoulders went up.

"Sure. Not all that well. Naomi was a pro and we dealt with her as one. Mary used to stop by at the end of the day to see Fred."

"He never talked to you about them?"

There was a moment during which Anthony had the look of a man about to lie. But he thought better of it. "No. We talked about everything else, but not that."

"His poetry?"

"Poetry?" A quizzical smile formed on Anthony's thin lips. The look of a man who thought his leg was being pulled.

"It doesn't matter."

"Did Fred write poetry?"

"He was a man of many parts. In some ways a man of mystery."

"You can say that again."

7 After she left Roger Knight Naomi told herself that talking with Roger Knight was just a little insurance before she talked with Tom. She would be equally frank with him this time. Two days ago she had been in Nashville, having covered the Tennessee game. Tom had called and just barked an order into the phone.

"I want to talk with you, and I mean now!"

"Tom?"

"It sure as hell isn't that leprechaun."

He slammed down the phone.

Naomi had been in the shower when the phone rang and she had wrapped herself in a towel and scampered into the bedroom, certain the phone would stop ringing before she got to it. If it was someone from the channel they would have called her cell phone so she had no idea who it might be. Once it might have been Fred. She had snatched up the phone to hear the irate voice of Tom.

What was wrong with him? It was one thing not to be an Irish fan but he seemed really to hate Notre Dame. It had been a mistake to introduce Fred to him.

"What a wimp," he had said afterward.

"He is not."

"God made Notre Dame Number One."
He said it with a sneer.

"Tom, he never said that."

"But he thinks so, doesn't he?"

"Well, you're nuts about the Cubs."

"It's my job."

"And Fred's job is Notre Dame sports information."

"It's not a job with those guys. It never is."

Of course she knew what underlay his rage. There is no one more bigoted than a fallen-away Catholic and Tom had plummeted like Lucifer from heaven when he fell in love with a twice-divorced woman and had been told there was no way in the world he could marry her in the church. That had been Lucille, long an item in the past, but Tom's bitterness on that occasion had not gone away. He had been an irregular attendant at Mass before that, but then he had sworn he would never enter a Catholic church again. He seemed to think he was punishing the church. Ever since, his attitude had hardened. He was a small-bore version of Julian the Apostate, not content simply not to believe. He had to

189

hate and oppose the thing he had left. And given Notre Dame's prominence in sports and the fact that it was the premier Catholic university in the nation, it followed as night the day that Tom must hate and loathe Notre Dame and everything — and everyone — connected with the university. All this had been clear as could be after the disastrous dinner at the Carriage House. Tom was programmed to hate Fred Neville.

"Where did Tom go?" Fred asked afterward.

"Loyola."

"Ah."

"No, that isn't it. He hates Loyola too."

"He sounds so cheerful announcing games."

"Some people do crossword puzzles."

He looked puzzled. But games are not the real world, their rules are arbitrary and absolute. Tom could occupy that world as a substitute for the world in which the rules had bitten him. She was glad she didn't have to explain this to Fred, but it seemed clear enough until she tried to express it.

Nor did it harm her theory that Tom took every occasion to come to South Bend and root for Notre Dame's opponent. The Lady Irish had flattened the opposition when he was here the weekend before last. He had asked for the use of the second bedroom in the channel's suite.

"Unless three would be a crowd."

"Tom, for heaven's sake."

"Well, how serious is it?"

"I'll keep you posted."

"Naomi, it would be the mistake of your lifetime."

A mistake she was finding it very difficult to make, as it happened. If there had been any doubt in Naomi's mind it was swept away when Fred had told her about the other woman.

"Who is she?"

"It doesn't matter."

"Meaning anyone else would do?"

"You know I don't mean that."

"You know I was a virgin, don't you?" Not wholly true, but this was love and war.

"Naomi . . ."

His moral sense was keen, his sense of honor wonderfully old-fashioned. It made him vulnerable to her unwillingness to shake hands and call it a day. In her darker moments she told herself that if she couldn't have him no one could.

It was Thelma the toothy secretary who had told Naomi about Mary Shuster, relishing the telling because she sensed that something had been going on between Naomi and Fred.

"Local girl?"

"Born and bred. Her father was on the faculty, she works in the registrar's office."

Naomi did not want to see Mary Shuster, but she could not quell her curiosity. When she saw her at the wake she knew who she was and after the funeral, at the university club, she had made the great mistake of picking a fight with her. Roger Knight and the old priest, Carmody, had saved her bacon, but Naomi had lost points with herself and that was more important than what others thought. Even so, she had wanted to talk to Roger Knight before catching her plane. That, she assured herself, had not been a mistake. How nice it would be to have the big fat professor in her corner. Sitting in her rented car outside the Knight apartment, she pressed her cheek against the window and was mesmerized by the lightly falling snow. As if for the first time she realized that Fred was gone for good. South Bend would never be the same again.

She took her cell phone from her purse and put through a call to Tom. The time was given digitally on the phone. So much for her flight from South Bend.

"Well, you lucked out there," he said.

"Where?"

"Fred."

"Tom, what a terrible thing to say."

"Or maybe not. You know you're in a bad spot, don't you?"

"I've lost the man I loved."

He made an obscene noise with his lips. "Have the police talked to you?"

"The police?"

"Naomi, think about it. Others must have known he was trying to dump you."

"Who told you that?"

"He did. The sonofabitch."

"When?"

"It doesn't matter. Can't you see the spot you're in? I hope you can account for your actions in those days before the body was found."

She sat in silence for a moment. "Tom, I can't believe we had the same parents."

"Still wearing Mom's ring?"

8 The first stop was the building in which Fred Neville had his apartment, for a confirmation from Santander.

"What is this?" Santander asked over the security chain when he had finally answered the door.

Stewart flourished a piece of paper. "Search warrant."

"You've already been in Neville's apartment. You're the only ones who can get into it."

"This is for your apartment."

Santander's eyes widened in apprehension. Who does not have secrets?

"Open up. We prefer not to break down doors."

The manager cursed in a language other than English, closed, then opened the door. A girl stood behind him terrified.

"Better get back to work, Teresa."

She scooted past Jimmy Stewart and Phil and disappeared up the stairs.

"Who's she?"

"One of the cleaning ladies."

"I sincerely hope so."

"Let me see that paper."

194

"First, a few questions."

"I don't have to answer any more questions."

"Would you rather be arrested for questioning?"

More oaths in his mother tongue.

"When was the last time you saw Neville?"

"I told you."

"Tell me again."

It was simply Stewart's way of softening him up. After fifteen minutes of hearing again what Santander had already told him, Stewart abruptly shifted.

"Why didn't you tell me that Naomi McTear had been to see him when he was supposedly missing?"

"Who?"

"Naomi McTear. You must have seen her on television."

Santander was clearly not following this. Stewart asked if he remembered being shown a photograph by Roger Knight.

"The fat guy?"

"Which you identified."

"I said she was the woman I saw go up to his apartment that Monday."

"You're sure?"

"Of course I'm sure. Why would I lie?"

"How long was she up there?"

"I only saw her go up. I don't keep track of people going in."

"She just walked in?"

"He had to let her in. You punch a button and the front door unlocks."

"So he must have been there to let her in."

"That's what I'm saying."

"And you just happened to look out your peephole and see her?"

"No. I was vacuuming the hall carpet."

"Had you ever seen her here before?"

"A couple times."

"But others could have been let in and you wouldn't know?"

"When I'm watching television I wouldn't hear the buzzer that goes off when the door is unlocked."

"What do you watch on television?"

"Sports. You know."

"So you must have seen Naomi McTear on television. She does what they call color. On cable."

"Yeah?"

"Maybe that's why you recognized her."

Santander shook his head vigorously. "No way. I had seen her here before. I didn't know who she was."

"You weren't curious about her?"

"What do you think I am?"

"What does Teresa think you are?"

"She's my niece, for God sakes."

So much for the high moral ground. They left Santander to wonder why he was being subjected to police harassment.

"He's telling the truth?" Stewart said.

"What do you think I am?" Phil was imitating Santander's strangled voice.

"Don't ask."

Scott Frye was on duty at the Hoosier Residences. He nodded when Stewart identified himself.

"I wondered when you'd get here."

"You prepared to confess?"

Scott's smirk disappeared and his mouth hung open. "Confess what?"

"Your sins. Isn't that what confession is?"

"I'm not a Catholic."

"Neither is my partner. This is Philip Knight. Another detective. Why did you think we would be coming here?"

"I didn't. I didn't mean that. It was just something to say."

"Pretty strange thing to say, wasn't it?"

"Yes. Yes, it was. Forget it."

"Pretty interesting too. Why would we come here?"

Scott was sweating now. He wasn't enjoying this at all.

"I don't know."

"Tell me what we ought to know."

"About what?"

"This place."

Scott seemed almost relieved to tell them about the condos, the apartments owned by wealthy Notre Dame alumni.

"Some rent them when they're not going to use them, but many are just there for when they come for a game. Media people stay here too."

"Media people."

"Reporters who come for the games."

"Television reporters?"

The sweat broke out again. He nodded.

"Like Naomi McTear?"

Bingo, Scott got out a handkerchief and mopped his forehead.

"That's why you expected us, isn't it?"

He nodded.

"Okay, tell us all about her."

"She's not here now. She left. This morning."

"This morning?"

"She stayed over."

"For what?"

"The funeral."

"What funeral?"

"Oh, come on."

"I want to know."

"She had been going out with the guy who was found dead."

"Fred Neville?"

"Yes."

"How do you know?"

"He stayed in her apartment!"

"You know that for a fact?"

"I know that for a fact." The impudent smirk with which he had greeted them was back.

"He stayed overnight?"

"That's right. They came in, drunk as owls and went up to the apartment and he didn't leave until morning. More than once."

"What kind of a place you running here?"

"If owners of condos want to have a friend in, there's nothing wrong."

"So why are you telling us this?"

Listening to all this, Phil thought that Stewart had a bit of a sadistic streak. He had Scott sweating bullets again.

"You asked me!"

"You got a key to the apartment?"

"You want to see it?"

"The key?"

"Come on."

"Show us," Stewart said.

The apartment was spick-and-span,

white carpet, white furniture, undistinguished paintings hanging on its white walls. Even the magazines on the coffee table were neatly arranged. *Sports Illustrated*, the *Blue and Gold*.

"She's a neat girl."

"The place has been cleaned. That's part of the condominium arrangement."

"Ah."

Scott suddenly struck his forehead. "You interested, I can show you what they cleaned out of here."

"What do you mean?"

"The girls take it out in plastic bags marked with the number of the apartment."

"Where is it?"

"I'll go get it."

"We'll go with you."

"You think I'm going to run away?"

"There's nothing here," Stewart said.

"Not anymore."

Phil had checked out the two bedrooms. The beds were made. In the bathroom there was nothing in the medicine cabinet except some toothpaste, a still-wrapped toothbrush, some throwaway razors and a small can of shaving cream. And deodorant.

"Anything?" Stewart asked Phil.

"Clean as a whistle."

Downstairs, Scott told them to wait in the lobby, he would fetch the plastic bag. Stewart just shook his head. They went out the back door and Scott led them to the Dumpster at the back of the lot, opened the lid. He began to pull out plastic bags, and put them on the packed snow around the Dumpster.

"What's the number of her apartment?"

Stewart had noticed the numbers stenciled on the bags. Scott's voice echoed in the opened bin.

"It's not here," Stewart said.

"That's all of them."

"You sure?"

"Take a look."

Stewart took a look. He turned to Scott. "Her room was cleaned?"

"That's right."

"So where's the bag?"

"You got me."

The back door opened and a girl came out. She was going to back in again but Stewart called her. She hugged herself as she came toward them. Stewart identified himself.

"Do you clean the apartments here?"

"Yes."

"We can't seem to find the sack from

number two-eleven."

The girl looked at Scott. "You asked for it."

Stewart turned to Scott.

"You already asked for the stuff taken out of Naomi McTear's apartment?"

"It wasn't her apartment. It belongs to the network."

"What did you do with it, Scott? Why did you want it?"

It was chilly out there but he was sweating again nonetheless. He glared at the girl. Then he tramped to a car, pressing a plastic thing he took from his pocket, and the trunk popped open. He stood aside so they could see the trash bag in the trunk.

"Well, well. My boy, you and the trash bag are going downtown."

"You're arresting me?"

"That's right."

The girl followed this with popped eyes. She hugged herself more tightly.

"I'm going inside."

"Thanks for your help," Stewart called after her.

9　The discovery of poison in the coffee cup from Fred Neville's apartment had excited even Boswell the coroner. But soon he subsided into his customary weltschmerz.

"It must have been self-administered."

"He just spooned a little strychnine into his coffee?"

"He put in some bourbon too."

"You never mentioned that before," Stewart said.

"I saw no reason to."

"Anything else you've found no reason to tell me?"

"Let's get going on the bag of trash."

For this little ceremony Stewart wanted Scott as one of the actors. On the way downtown, Scott had given one unconvincing excuse after another as to why he had put the bag from the apartment where Naomi McTear had been staying in the trunk of his car.

"You kinky or something?"

"Just curious."

"I couldn't agree more."

But Stewart was weary of badgering people. It was too easy to make Scott sweat and Santander could be played like a musical instrument. But when they got around to the trash bag, he asked Scott to empty it.

"I wouldn't want to deprive you of the thrill."

The bag contained what one might expect. You would have thought Naomi McTear had a cold, there was so much used tissue in the sack. But when Scott brought out the little container, Jimmy Stewart held out an open plastic baggie to him. "Just drop it in here. Are your fingerprints registered?"

"My fingerprints!"

"Were you ever in the service?"

That was a diversion, more badgering. Stewart handed the baggie to Boswell, who squinted at it, held it up to the light, turned it to read the legend on the container.

"This is the poison. Strychnine."

"How did you know, Scott?"

"I didn't. Honest to God, I didn't."

"How often do you confiscate trash bags and put them in the trunk of your car? More importantly, when did you put this container in the bag?"

That wasn't badgering, only the obvious question. And it gave Stewart an excuse to put Scott in the slammer.

"You got a lawyer?"

"Why would I need a lawyer?"

"You do now. Better get one."

He booked Scott, let him make a phone call, and turned him over to the turnkey. "Who did you call?"

"A friend."

"Is he a lawyer?"

"He'll know what to do."

They took Scott away. Stewart went back to Boswell and Phil Knight. Boswell said, "You really think he did it?"

"I don't think. I'm a cop. The man had the bag, the bag contained the poison, what's to think about?"

"Dinner?" Phil said.

"Good idea."

"I'll call Roger."

So dinner was arranged at the Knights' apartment. Phil went on home and Stewart said he would be there as soon as he could. He wanted to see who the friend was that Scott had called.

It was Anthony Boule, Fred Neville's assistant at the Joyce Center. That was a bit of a surprise, not that Stewart showed it.

"You his partner or something?" he asked Anthony before they brought Scott from his cell.

"I know him," Anthony said carefully.
"He had one call and he called you."
"He's not thinking clearly."
"You know any lawyers?"
"Is he going to need one?"
"Let him tell you."

Roger had made lasagna and Phil opened a bottle of red and they spent the evening talking about where they were. Roger was wearing a huge white apron and had a baseball cap on his head. The servings he dished out were king-size of course, but he had made enough lasagna for three such servings apiece. It was a mystery that Phil did not weigh as much as his brother, eating as he did.

"It is a relief that no one can now think that Fred took his own life," Roger said.

"Boswell said he might have self-administered the poison."

"As did Socrates."

Jimmy Stewart and Phil observed a moment of silence. Such enigmatic remarks were best not responded to.

"Of course he knew he was doing it," Roger added.

"Fred?"

"Socrates."

"Ah."

"Now we know we are looking for the one who killed Fred. What motive would this fellow Scott have?"

"He's a friend of Anthony Boule."

Roger found this interesting. "Who was not satisfied playing second fiddle to Fred."

"The removal of an impediment?"

"But Scott himself drew attention to the trash bag. Would you have thought of it otherwise?"

"No."

"Unless he is blowing the whistle on Anthony."

"And called him to make sure we would see the connection?" Phil said.

"The trash came from the apartment Naomi McTear had been in," Stewart reminded the brothers.

"God knows she had a motive."

Phil spelled it out, relying on what Roger had told him as well as what Stewart would already know. The case against Naomi was certainly strong. She had been identified as the woman who visited Fred in his apartment the day before the body was found. That accorded with the coroner's guess on the time of death. The container of poison had been found in the trash taken from her apartment. Motive?

Fred was trying to give her the heave-ho and she was resisting. Her claim to be engaged to Fred seemed well-founded.

"The Nevilles accepted her as such."

"Are they still in town?" Roger asked.

"Mrs. Neville said they would stay until their son was actually buried."

"No need to put that off any longer, is there?"

Stewart shook his head. "There never really was any need to do that. I had hoped it might smoke out whoever had done it."

"So you never thought it was suicide?"

"It was or it wasn't. If it wasn't I didn't want whoever did it to think that it was all six feet under."

Phil said, "So where is Naomi?"

Jimmy Stewart said, "I'll find out. Her employer should know."

"What do you think, Roger?"

"I think she's in Chicago."

"I meant what do you think of Naomi as a killer?"

"Anyone can do anything, of course." This was Roger's rock-bottom theory. He dismissed all talk of criminal types, as if wrongdoers were a special breed. In his view anyone could, in the proper circumstances, and with slow antecedent weakening, do anything, no matter how horrible. Why else do those who knew serial killers describe them as choirboys?

"So Naomi could have done this?"

"She could have, yes."

"But you don't think so."

"Scott could have done it. Anthony could have done it." His voice dropped. "Mary could have done it."

"Oh, I doubt that, Roger."

"So do I. And I doubt that Naomi killed the man she wouldn't let go."

This led to a free-for-all discussion in the course of which both Stewart and Phil became more and more convinced that Naomi had done it. She could not let Fred go and she could not keep him either. The prospect of Mary Shuster walking Fred down the aisle was more than she could handle. She snapped.

"If not me, no one," Phil summed it up.

Roger pursed his lips. "Maybe."

When Stewart left he told Roger, "Until you can come up with a plausible alternative, it's Naomi as far as I'm concerned. Top priority is to find her and have a long talk."

The following morning, Jimmy Stewart called. "Do you get the *Trib*, Roger?"

"The local one?"

"Is there another?"

"It's probably on the Web."

"Anyway, we now know where Naomi McTear is."

"Where?"

"In Fred Neville's apartment. Dead."

PART FOUR

TURN OF THE SCREW

I Santander, perhaps understandably less civic-minded than he had been before being questioned by Stewart, had not immediately telephoned the police when he noticed the unfamiliar car parked in Fred Neville's space. The tape had been removed from the doorway of Neville's apartment and the police vigil ended. It was the building manager's intention to talk with the woman about whom Stewart had show so much curiosity. To this end, he left the chained door of his own apartment ajar so that he might surprise her when she came out. He had noticed the car at midday and kept sentry duty throughout the afternoon, taking time out for hurried visits to the bathroom. Had she slipped away? But the car was still in Neville's parking place. Finally, he switched from passive to active mode and went upstairs and knocked on the door.

He stepped back, to provide a better view through the peephole, and waited. The door was not opened. He knocked again, more loudly. Again, nothing. He went downstairs and called Stewart.

When Stewart came he was alone and

Santander went unimpeded up the stairs after him. Stewart turned.

"You got a master key?"

Santander handed it to him.

"You used this?"

"From time to time."

"On this door, today?"

"No!"

Stewart pounded on the door with the full weight of police authority but as with Santander's earlier effort there was no response. He put the key in the lock and opened the door.

She was on the couch, slumped over, a cup of coffee on the table before her. Stewart stood in front of her, then looked at her from other vantage points, and took out a cell phone.

The routine in such matters is long-established. Touch nothing, move carefully, wait for the medical examiner. The coffee cup on the table prepared Stewart for Boswell's initial verdict.

"Ditto."

"Poison?"

"Looks like it."

Wearing rubber gloves, Boswell picked up the cup and smelled it. "Liquor too."

"Irish coffee."

The body was left where it had been

found, once Boswell unnecessarily pronounced the woman dead. A crew from
the police lab was in the wings but before
giving way to them Boswell had a question.

"Who was she?"

"Naomi McTear."

Boswell crouched and stared intently at
the face that had come to rest against an
arm of the couch. "I should have recognized her."

"You never saw her dead before."

"I never saw her alive. Live, maybe, on
television. But never in the flesh."

The word had an odd resonance in the
circumstances. The police team took over.
They were three, one stout woman named
Benson, a dwarflike one named Hedges,
and Farwell, who looked young enough to
be Benson's son. Stewart took Hedges with
him into the kitchen.

"Better check the coffee cannister."

"We'll check everything."

"Just don't forget that."

Stewart called Phil Knight to say he was
coming over. Roger answered, Phil wasn't
there, but Stewart would settle for Roger.

Roger said, "She must have gone there
after leaving me. She had said she was

going to the airport."

"Why would she go there and make coffee and relax with a cup?"

"Sentimental visit?"

"Any indication she might do that when you talked to her?"

"When she left it was to catch a flight."

"So much for her as a suspect."

Roger had never thought much of that idea but he would have preferred it to be disproved in a less tragic fashion.

The coffee in the cannister taken from Fred's kitchen proved to be liberally mixed with the poison that had killed first Fred and then Naomi. Stewart was understandably angry that he hadn't thought of the cannister but Roger consoled him. After all, his theory had been that Naomi visited Fred and, presumably, doctored his Irish coffee because she was so distraught over his desire to set her aside. Things were not simplified by the fact that the container of poison had been found in the trash bag taken from the network apartment Naomi had been occupying.

"If she put that stuff into Fred's coffee cannister, she wasn't likely to make a pot of coffee from it."

The police mind has to assume that life is rational, however criminal. Effects have causes and when the causes are people they have reasons for what they do. Of course in the real world what we do often has unforeseen consequences and of these the agent acts in ignorance. No need to tell Jimmy Stewart that it was not at all impossible that Naomi had been preoccupied and had not considered what she was doing. Such things happen every day.

When Phil came, he listened to the news of Naomi's death with a stoic expression on his face. But his mind was working.

"So who's left?"

He meant who could have poisoned Fred deliberately and Naomi unintentionally? The fact that the poison had been found in Naomi's trash bag became the focus of attention. Scott was still being held and the three went downtown to talk with him. Scott's story that he had sequestered the trash bag for no reason and stashed it in the trunk of his car was inherently implausible. His protest that he had told Stewart about the bag was countered with the undeniable truth that it was the appearance of the girl from the cleaning crew that had prompted Scott to open the trunk.

"If I knew that poison was in there, I wouldn't have done it."

"What did you expect to find in it?"

"I don't know. I want a lawyer."

"I thought you might. Your friend Anthony should have told you to do that."

"Anthony?" Roger said.

"Anthony Boule."

Roger's eyes widened, but then the thought he had been having reasserted itself.

"Did Naomi's brother ever use the apartment?"

"Yes!" Scott was delighted with the question. "He was there that week. I talked baseball with him and one night he asked us up to watch the Blackhawks with him."

"Us?"

"Me. Anthony. The girl from the Joyce Center with the big teeth."

"Thelma?"

Scott nodded.

"Why the hell didn't you mention this before?" Stewart demanded.

"It's why I wanted the trash."

During the game Tom McTear had drunk deep and become expansive. Scott said it was like having him give a personal play-by-play for them. And he had diagrammed various plays. "That's what I wanted. What a souvenir."

"They weren't in the bag."

"Anthony took them when we left, the sonofagun."

Roger said to Stewart, "I think you better have a talk with Tom McTear."

2   The deaths of Fred Neville and then Naomi McTear brought out another side of Roger Knight, and Griselda wasn't so sure she liked it. Why should he waste his brain wondering about why something or other had happened. There were zillions of such events every day and getting immersed in one of them seemed arbitrary.

"Fred was my friend," Roger said.

"I don't mean they shouldn't find who did it and punish them but why should you spend your time on it?"

"Stick to important things?"

"Yes."

"Shadows and images."

Griselda didn't understand so he told her of Plato's cave and his emerging theory that the things of this world were not real, just pale copies of the really real which was outside space and time. The philosopher's task was to wean himself from the things of this world and occupy himself only with the eternal and changeless.

"It sounds religious."

"Just what some of the Church fathers

thought. But in many ways it is antithetical to Christianity."

Like it or not, our lives are lived in a river of change and contingency from which truths are plucked, some likely, some highly probable, a few necessary. The mind enables us to transcend change in this way, but we are not mere minds. The mind is a capacity of a bodily creature, and our minds couldn't work without the constant sensory reports of those fleeting and temporal events.

"I have always found it impossible not to have a body," Roger said.

Griselda laughed. "Okay. I'm wrong. So who did it?"

"Who is your suspect?"

"Mine?"

"Someone put poison in the coffee cannister in Fred Neville's kitchen. It killed him and Naomi as well."

"What was she doing there?"

"The important question is who else was in that apartment?"

"I was."

"You?"

"The night he took me to dinner at Parisi's for the big pep talk we stopped there so he could check his telephone messages."

"Were there any?"

"I didn't eavesdrop."

"I wish you had. The microcassette on which calls were recorded is missing from his phone."

Griselda shook her head. "I never thought of Fred Neville as a man of mystery. Now all these things begin to seem important."

"Everyone's a mystery. Who else could have been there?"

"Mary Shuster, I suppose. And people from the Joyce Center."

"Anthony?"

"He was his assistant, more or less."

"How well do you know him?"

"Anthony?" Griselda made a face. "He is very ambitious."

"For Fred's job?"

"If he thought he would get that . . ." She stopped. "Do you think that Anthony did it?"

Roger shrugged. "I think lots of people could have done it. You, for example."

"Me!"

"Say you resented more than you let on Fred's effort to keep you on the team. Maybe he misbehaved when you were in his apartment. This is how the police think. Lots of motives could be imagined.

So you decide to give him the coup de grâce."

"The coo de what?"

"You poison him."

"I don't even like you imagining me doing something like that."

"Oh there are many other candidates."

Roger did not tell Griselda of the possibility that Naomi's brother was the one behind it all. He had little doubt that Tom McTear would soon emerge as Jimmy Stewart's number-one suspect. It might take a flight of fancy to put Griselda in the role of serial poisoner, but Naomi during her visit with Roger before leaving ostensibly to catch a plane had told him startling things about her brother's attitude toward Fred. *Hatred* was not too strong a word. All of McTear's negative feelings toward Notre Dame and the church had found their single focus in Fred Neville. Opportunity? He had been in town, the poison was found in the trash taken from the apartment where he had stayed in the second bedroom. Fred's apartment? Naomi must have had a key, she had let herself in on the fateful day she had made a lethal cup of Irish coffee.

3 Tom McTear drove to South Bend after the call from Stewart came, doing eighty on the toll road and ready to plead an emergency if he were stopped. But he breezed through unticketed in less than two hours, communicating with Stewart along the way, the detective having made the mistake of giving Naomi's brother the number of his cell phone. He was told to come to Fred Neville's apartment and Stewart noticed that he did not ask for the address or directions to it. The body was still on the premises when he arrived and at the sight of Naomi he broke down, sobbing helplessly, wanting to take her in his arms.

"The poor little girl," he said again and again. For him Naomi remained the little sister of long ago and the sight of her dead did not change that.

Stewart had not conveyed the apparent cause of death to McTear over the phone, and the location of the body had brought a profane reaction. "In Neville's apartment? What in hell was she doing there?"

"We're looking into it."

"What do you mean?"

The signal was lost and Stewart turned off his phone. But McTear dissolved at the sight of his sister. Ten minutes after he got there, the body was transferred to a body bag and McTear let out a cry and went into the kitchen.

"Is that coffee fresh?"

"It's evidence."

McTear looked at him.

"Everything in the apartment is potential evidence."

"Can I have a cup of evidence?"

"I told you the medical examiner's preliminary cause of death."

McTear looked at the carafe of coffee with dread. "My God."

"Where will you be staying?"

He thought about it. "Do you know the Hoosier Residences?"

"Sure."

"I have to get word to the family. And make arrangements." He suppressed a sob.

"There's plenty of time. There will be an autopsy."

McTear turned a tragic look on Stewart. "My God, this is awful."

Opinions would vary on McTear's behavior when he first saw the dead body of his little sister. No acting had been required to express his grief and horror. That, it was conceded, was genuine. But his reaction to Naomi's death was perfectly compatible with his having been the one who put the poison in the coffee cannister. It was the scene in the kitchen that caused two schools of thought to form. The one held that he was genuinely surprised and would have poured himself a cup of the poisoned coffee if Stewart had not stopped him. Nonsense, the other school maintained. During his speedy but still long drive from Chicago he must have figured out what had happened. When he arrived he was told of the coffee Naomi had drunk. That was fresh in his mind when he put on the performance in the kitchen. If anything, it drew attention to him, as if by what he had done he was seeking to bring about the fallacious reasoning that characterized the first school.

Laura Reith emerged as Tom McTear's champion in the press. In her signature battle dress, she told the camera that the local police were persecuting the voice of the Cubs.

Belonging not quite to either school, Roger felt obliged to convey what Naomi had told him when visiting him on what would turn out to be the day she died.

"If he hates Notre Dame so much what was McTear always doing in town?"

"The last time? Baseball. He was checking out Maneri on some pro prospects the Cubs are interested in."

True enough, as it happened, but that single-purpose explanation did not jibe with Scott's claim that Tom McTear had been a regular at the Hoosier Residences.

The chastened desk clerk had been released, having saved himself attorney's fees. But he was mindful that he had been let go because of the growing suspicion that Tom McTear had done away with his sister's beau and unwittingly with her.

"He must have put that package in the trash," Scott said.

"Too bad for him you decided to put that bag in your trunk."

"In a way I'm sorry about that. I told you what I was looking for. I don't wish him any harm, you know."

But the news of Naomi's death was of national interest, given her prominence on cable television. There was more than a hint in several stories that Tom had been questioned by the police and that he had been no friend of his sister's boyfriend. That the dead couple had been engaged now went uncontested. For such a sports celebrity as Tom to

227

be written of in this way was hardly a matter of indifference, and he demanded that Stewart spike these rumors.

"Just tell the media you're innocent."

He had done that, of course, in an interview with Laura Reith, but the reporter's crusade had not caught on with her colleagues in the media.

"No. That would only give credit to these wild guesses."

"So what do you want me to do?"

"Find out who did this," Tom pleaded.

"I would like a little cooperation from you."

"Cooperation! I came down here like a shot, I have been at your disposal ever since arriving, what more do you want?"

"Less interference from your lawyer. Every time I ask you a question, he puts the kibosh on it."

"Ask me anything."

"You mean it?"

"Of course I mean it."

"Sure you don't want your lawyer present?"

"To hell with him."

Maurice Gibbons, a suave and gifted lawyer from Chicago who, among other clients, had the Chicago Cubs, would not have appreciated this summary dismissal.

But it was an opportunity not to be disdained, so Jimmy Stewart and Philip Knight were closeted with McTear, but not until a little flare-up about Phil's presence was settled.

"He's not a South Bend detective?"

Phil said, "I represent the university."

"Notre Dame? What do they have to do with this?"

"You're kidding, right? You know where Fred worked."

"And you objected to my having Gibbons here."

"You want to give him a call?"

"No. Let's get on with it."

They got on with it, starting with the fact that Tom had been staying in the Hoosier Residences network apartment with his sister. He seemed surprised they knew that. And he was clearly unprepared for the news that in the trash bag from that apartment had been found a container of the poison that had killed Fred Neville and Naomi.

"That seemed to point the finger at her," said Stewart.

"Naomi?"

"Maybe it still does. There seems to have been a falling-out between your sister and Neville."

"I told her what I thought of him."

"You didn't like him."

McTear hesitated. "I suppose you get used to it in this town, but Notre Dame fans can be a pain in the rear, and nobody works for them who isn't a fan. How can you be objective if you're already committed to the view that a team is God's gift to the world?"

"Is that how Fred felt?"

"They all feel that way. I've seen it for years."

"Do you think it is possible your sister put that poison in Neville's coffee cannister and then mistakenly made a pot of coffee from it?"

"That's an awful question to have to answer."

"What is the answer?"

"I don't know. You're asking me if my sister was a murderer."

"There is another possibility, McTear. You could have put that poison in Neville's coffee."

"Oh, sure. Just dropped in and loaded up his coffee."

"It could have been done."

"Tell me, what made you look into the trash from that apartment?"

"That was courtesy of a fan of yours."

McTear lowered his chin and stared at Stewart. "A fan?"

"Fellow named Scott. He is a desk clerk at the Hoosier Residences."

McTear was nodding.

"Apparently you had him and some of his friends up to the apartment to watch a game. You diagrammed some plays and he hoped to find them in the trash."

"Did he?"

"A guy named Anthony swiped them before Scott got to them, though."

"The one from the sports information department?"

"That's right."

"If he had asked, I would have given them to Scott."

"If you had, he wouldn't have swiped the bag and then been forced to tell us he had put it in the trunk of his car."

"Forced."

"One of the cleaning maids . . ."

A man may well wonder about the tremendous odds against things happening as they actually do. Tom McTear had little inclination to philosophy nor indeed to general theories, outside the realm of sports. But he wore a stricken look as he considered the implications of what Phil had told him.

"I didn't do this. I didn't like Neville, but it was impersonal. He could have been any mad Irish fan. And I don't mean, if not me then Naomi. Whatever else, she liked the guy. Really. I talked to her like an uncle, but to no effect. I probably strengthened her in her determination to marry him."

"The obstacle seems to have been on the other side."

Tom waved away this objection. "Naomi always got what she wanted."

Stewart told Tom he appreciated his sentiments but the fact remained that the container of poison had been found in the trash bag taken from the apartment in Hoosier Residences shared by the two McTears.

"It looks like it had to be one or the other of you."

"What about this guy Scott?"

"What about it?"

"If he took the bag he might have dumped the container in it."

"That's possible, of course. But unlike you and your sister, he seems to have no motivation."

McTear looked from Phil to Stewart. His mouth became a thin line. "I better call Gibbons."

4 Mary Shuster wondered what else could happen to make a fool of her. She first heard of the death of Naomi McTear from Roger Knight and he urged her to come to them that night, with her mother. It was a welcome suggestion, but it only underscored that Mary was in need of special comfort now. For all that, before going to the Knights' apartment, she detoured by the grotto and offered a prayer for her rival. How almost ghoulish it all now seemed. She and Naomi had been contesting for a man who was now dead. And so soon afterward, Naomi had followed him into that bourne from which no traveler returns. I alone have escaped to tell you? But it was Roger Knight who had given her the news.

"When? Where?"

"I'll tell you everything we know when you get here."

"But where did it happen?"

"In South Bend."

She did not pursue it, warned by something in his tone. She steeled herself for more bad news. Of course she had realized at the wake and funeral that many regarded her as demented. Dressing all in black had seemed the least she could do when she realized that Fred was gone. Of course she was making a statement, but she had not imagined that Naomi would show up. Why couldn't the woman understand that Fred meant it when he told her their relationship was through?

The problem was he was too gentle. Mary herself had often sensed his malleability and had to restrain herself from leading him down paths he would not himself have gone. Her great regret was that she had not balked when the question of keeping their engagement secret had arisen. She had reasons of her own, petty reasons, reasons that could easily have been set aside, but his concerned Naomi. She was sure now she could have overpowered him on that matter, insisted that a secret engagement was as good as no engagement at all. A notice in the paper would have sufficed. Naomi would only have embarrassed herself taking exception to that. And now Naomi too was dead.

From the grotto, Mary walked back across the campus to Notre Dame Village, dreading what would be told her there, yet eager to learn. It was far worse than she could have imagined.

Before telling her, Roger got her settled and put a glass of red wine in her hand.

"Are you making pasta?"

"Of course. Phil is picking up your mother."

"Tell me everything before she gets here."

"Come help."

The kitchen was like a sauna, a huge kettle of water aboil on the stove, sending up clouds of steam. Roger insisted on a volcanic cauldron before putting in the pasta.

Mary listened with wonder, dread and finally foreboding. Roger told her of Naomi's stopping by when she was ostensibly headed for the airport.

"She must have gone from here to Fred's apartment."

"The police let her in?"

"The police had withdrawn."

Silence. "The building manager?"

The steam did not conceal Roger's agonized expression as he shook his head.

"So she let herself in."

"I don't want to put the garlic bread in the oven until your mother and Phil get here."

"She had a key."

What a racing riot of thoughts the realization brought. Had Fred really been as weak as that, telling her one thing and Naomi another. How had he spoken of her to Naomi?

"What exactly happened to her?"

"She brewed some coffee. The poison that killed Fred was mixed with the coffee in the cannister."

"Dear God."

"I will never forgive myself for not thinking of that. At the time, Naomi's visit the day before he died drove other possibilities from my mind."

"You thought she had done it?"

"A woman scorned." He began to feed pasta into the boiling water. Boil, boil, toil and trouble.

Whoever had poisoned the coffee had not intended to kill Naomi, but what if Fred had served coffee to others, using the contents of that cannister? It had stood there in the kitchen like a time bomb that could go off anytime, but certainly at sometime, and the one who had put it there could then be far away.

"Who?"

"Suspicion has turned on her brother Tom."

"Oh."

"He was more eager than Fred that she

should end the relationship."

Mary thought about that. Perhaps Fred had not been as forceful as he might have been, but he had tried to clear things up before they announced their engagement.

"Why did he hate Fred?"

"He hated Notre Dame. It's a long story."

"So it wouldn't matter where he was when Fred died?"

"No. There's more. A container of the poison was found in the trash taken from the apartment where he had been staying with his sister."

"Has he been arrested?"

"Detained for questioning, in the phrase. He has gotten a lawyer."

Was that to be the resolution of these terrible events? Mary could summon no sense of satisfaction that the one who had killed Fred would be brought to justice. Fred would still be dead, and Naomi too. For a fleeting moment she envied her rival and then the painful thoughts came. What would people make of the fact that Naomi had been able to let herself into Fred's apartment? Despite the fact that Naomi's death was accidental, it had the look of throwing herself on the pyre of her lost be-loved. That would seem to negate Mary's claim to have been Fred's fiancée. People would talk, but nothing would be said in her presence, not that she knew what she could say in response. She had become a ridiculous figure indeed. When she said this, Roger gave the boiling pasta a stir with a wooden spoon and then took her in his arms.

"You know that Fred loved you. Remember his poem."

Mary nodded. There was that. She could bear the public humiliation as long as she could cling to the coded poem he had written for her, declaring his love for Mary Shuster. Despite that, perhaps because of it, she wept and Roger, a veritable mountain of security, rocked her in his arms. He stepped back at the sound of the bell.

"Would you let them in, Mary?"

5 Anthony found Scott a different man from the one he had seen at police headquarters. Then Scott had been chastened, bewildered, no longer the cocky cynic, fearful. Now, released, his old sarcasm had returned along with his smirky smile. And there was a scarcely suppressed air of triumph.

"You're a writer," he informed Anthony.

"Of press releases."

Scott dismissed this. "You can handle the language, that's all I need. I've had the idea of the half century. Ready? What has happened is the stuff of which books are made. You and I are going to tell all. You must know how to go about it."

Anthony's first reaction was that such a book would put him in another league than Fred Neville. He was still competing with Fred, dead though he might be. But second thoughts came swiftly.

"I don't think the university would want to keep drawing attention to what happened to Fred."

"Fred! He has only a minor role. Think of it. We have a nationally-known TV personality, we have the color man for the

Cubs. Fred is the bone of contention between them. I am sure that Tom McTear will cooperate with us."

"In jail?"

"All the better. The condemned man tells all."

Laura Reith had been to Hoosier Residences, asking around, and Scott feared the reporter would have the same idea he had.

It was a great idea, Anthony admitted that, and they began to talk about how it could be done. First, they must find a publisher. Of course the university press was out. It occurred to Anthony again that to go ahead with this would endanger his own position at the Joyce Center. No need to dwell on that now. He would play it by ear. He could discuss it with Thelma; she had the shrewdness necessary to veto the idea if she thought it would be the end of him. Thelma's interest in him was suddenly an asset. But for the moment he sat and eagerly conspired with Scott on how they would jointly attain fame and fortune.

"My first thought was to give you hell for stealing those pages Tom scribbled the night we were all in the apartment watching the Blackhawks. Now they can figure in the book. That will be a big chapter, underlining our central role. My finding the container of poison in the trash is of course the turning point."

Anthony could see that Scott might be a difficult partner to work with. There was something of condescension in the way he addressed Anthony, as if he were merely a writing machine, an instrument of his idea, a junior partner. For a fleeting moment Anthony understood Thelma's resentment at being the doormat of the office. But he said nothing. After all, he did have those pages of Tom McTear's.

"Why do it with him?" Thelma said, moving her teeth thoughtfully on her lower lip.

"It's his idea."

"He couldn't do anything with it. You have the writing skills." She laid a long-fingered hand on his sleeve, as if to show the absence of ring. Anthony grew cautious.

"If the university heard I was doing this I would be out on my ear."

"Sweetie, if you do this you won't need the university."

Anthony felt alarm. Life apart from Notre Dame seemed a species of death.

"I'll help you," Thelma said.

"And then there's Mary."

Thelma's hand gripped his arm tightly. "What about her?"

"Think of what she's been through."

Thelma pushed away from him, rolling back behind her desk. "You really are as bad as Fred Neville."

"What do you mean?"

But immediately she softened. "Nothing."

"It would be a ratty thing to go ahead without Scott. It was his idea."

"Ideas are a dime a dozen. It's the execution that counts. I meant it when I said I'd help you."

For the second time in an hour Anthony was plotting the book, this time with a different collaborator. He assured Thelma she would get twin billing.

"Does that mean I pay twice?" She nudged him.

"Joint authorship."

Impulsively she kissed his cheek. "Okay, partner."

It turned out that Thelma had taken a course in creative writing at IUSB, the local campus of the state university, and was a font of publishing lore. They would need an agent, that was essential. Getting to a publisher with an idea involved jumping more hurdles than a track meet.

"We'll check it out in *LMP*, they're all listed there."

"What's *LMP*?"

"Not Lady Make Partner. *Literary Market Place*. A reference book. They have it at the library." She brightened, pulled the phone toward her with one hand and pulled the directory from a drawer with the other. In a minute, she was on the phone to the library and was put through to a person who could help. She explained what she needed. She listened.

"Call me back, would you? Thelma Maynooth." She gave her number.

While they waited, she had Anthony block it out, the parts, the chapters, photographs they would want. Anthony could feel his creative juices begin to flow. He thought of Scott and suppressed the memory. He did remember that it was Thelma who had indicated that he should take the pages Tom McTear had written on while he explained hockey and baseball to them. Maybe they had become partners that night. A soothing thought. That made Scott seem an interloper.

The phone rang. "Thelma."

Her eyes rolled upward and she exposed her teeth. "Can I take a message, Scott? I have to leave this phone open."

She nodded, murmuring affirmatively as she listened, then put down the phone. Almost immediately it rang. Rose at the library had *LMP* open before her. A lengthy conversation ensued, with Thelma taking rapid notes. Anthony got up and went to Fred's office. The door was closed, but not locked. He went inside and shut the door behind him and was enclosed by the absence of Fred. He went around the desk and sat, imagining himself as Fred's successor. But the book idea would put an end to such thoughts. That realization, plus the sense of treachery going ahead without Scott gave him, convinced him he had to call a halt before Thelma went too far.

The seat he sat in was both comfortable and upright and wheeled easily about. He turned this way and that, looked at Fred's framed Notre Dame diploma, at the plaques and awards he had received. It was a depressing thought that those walls would be largely bare if this were his office. He could put up his Boston College diploma, a conversation piece that could lead into talk about Frank Leahy.

The door opened and Thelma came in, closing the door with a practiced bump of her hip. She was studying the notes she had. Then she looked up at Anthony sitting at the desk.

"Well don't you look pretty."

"Thelma, I'm having doubts."

She came and sat on the desk. "Of course you are. This is a big step. But it's a step into the big time. Let's go over what I've learned."

There seemed little harm in that. Sometimes the best way to handle temptation was not vigorous rejection but parrying it by apparently giving in.

Thelma called what she thought was the most promising agent on the list and conducted the conversation herself. Anthony might have objected, feeling for a moment as he had with Scott, but it was better this way. The responsibility seemed to devolve upon Thelma. No need to tell her right away about his doubts. She was tantalizingly indirect when she talked with the agent, not wanting to give away too much, just enough to be tantalizing.

"It's a Notre Dame sports book with a difference." The magic words. The shelves in the bookstore groaned under Notre Dame titles but they sold like candy and not just on game weekends. Alumni were scattered across the country, almost all of them potential buyers of such a book.

"You appreciate that we have to be cautious. Who's *we?* Just say it is someone in the athletic department. Of course I'm calling from Notre Dame."

Once again she was making notes. Fifteen minutes later, having parried the agent's efforts to know more, she hung up.

"Here's what we do. First, a one-page statement of the thesis of the book. Second, a rough indication of the chapters. When you get those done I'll fax them off to him and we could know in hours if it will fly."

Again a point was reached when he should dash cold water on the idea. But Thelma had already gone to so much trouble and that seemed cruel. Besides there was no guarantee that the agent would be able to place the idea.

"Use Fred's computer, but don't store anything. Caution is the watchword."

She got off the desk and looked down at him with her arms folded. Anthony decided that she wasn't all that bad-looking, or maybe he was just used to her. And it was hard not to be impressed with the way she had taken the ball and run with it. Again, she kissed his cheek, putting her arms around his neck.

"Fred always kept the door open when I was in here with him."

The remark hung in the air after she had left, urging him to get going. When he had something printed out they would talk about it. Thelma was a flirt, no doubt of that. And he himself had only been a target of opportunity before. When Fred was around, it was for him that she had batted her lashes.

6 Throughout these events the Lady Irish basketball schedule had gone on and Griselda's play improved once she had managed to drive from her mind that Fred Neville had been poisoned and now Naomi McTear too. On the floor, with the roar of the crowd, and life reduced to the task of getting down the floor and directing the team's play, she outdid herself. They played in Ann Arbor, they played Creighton in Omaha, they returned home for a game against Purdue. Everywhere it was Griselda who was first sought out by reporters after the game, and who at Muffin McGraw's side made the self-effacing statements expected of a star. Basketball was a team game, it was the team that won or lost. But flying home, her mind would be filled again with what Roger Knight had told her. Both he and his brother were tied up in the making of the case against Tom McTear and she was lucky to get a few minutes with him after class.

"You almost convince me Egan is a better novelist than I thought."

In a paper, Griselda had compared him

with the early James and Howells, and Egan came off well from the comparison.

"I'd rather read him than Howells."

"Have you read *Indian Summer*?"

"Is that an assignment?"

"I think he was imitating James. Much of the story takes place in Europe."

"Tell me about the other thing."

He knew immediately what she meant. "It looks as if they are going to indict Tom McTear. Gibbons has been stalling the decision but he is running out of tricks."

"What will happen to him?"

"There's no certainty they can get a conviction."

"Do you think he did it?"

He thought for a moment. "Only every other day."

"I'd like to make an appointment."

"I'll call you, all right?"

"Sure."

She told herself that he hadn't meant it as a put-down but that is the way she felt. Back in her room she called Mary Shuster and asked how she was holding up.

"It's very lonely."

"I imagine."

"And I suppose you're very busy."

"Not too busy to take a break at the Huddle."

★ ★ ★

The Huddle is the original non-refectory eating place at Notre Dame, housed in an old building that had once contained the science department in which the Zahm brothers had sought to provide a more balanced education to students, lest they think that the liberal arts made up the whole of higher education. The building had been doubled in size in recent years, with the original architecture retained and a fair facsimile of the brick once made of the mud that St. Mary's lake employed. To the naked and uninstructed eye it seemed in its entirety a nineteenth-century building. Like most of the older buildings on campus, it had known a number of uses, until it finally metamorphosed into the student center. The aroma of sizzling burgers emanated from it, riding the chill November air, but inside there was a choice of high-cholesterol foods, Asian and Italian as well as the mandatory hamburgers and fries. Clean it might be, at least several times a day, but it could not be called well-lighted.

Griselda loaded up a tray, hers the appetite of an athlete, but Mary settled for coffee, and they took a table away from the roar of the huge and distorting television screen.

"You won again last night," Mary said.

The Lady Irish had yet to be defeated, but Griselda did not point this out.

"I've just come from Professor Knight's class."

"What a comfort he has been to me and my mother."

"And now they have the man who did it."

"He can't have imagined that his sister too would die."

Silence, or as much silence as could be expected in the Huddle. Then Mary said, "You know she was found dead in Fred Neville's apartment."

"Roger told me."

Mary's eyes were moist. "That was the final crushing blow. It has made me doubt that I ever really knew Fred."

"He loved you."

"So he said. But did he go on saying the same to her? She was able to let herself into his apartment, and that means —"

"Only that she had a key," Griselda said briskly. "Besides, you know what she was like."

"I didn't know her at all. She was just the name of a problem for Fred and me."

"No one in the Joyce Center thought that theirs was anything more than what

251

you would expect between a sports-information person and a reporter."

"Is that true?"

"We were more likely to think it was Thelma and Fred."

"Thelma!"

"I know. A real Flirty Gertie. She is one of those women who are always touching men, laying a hand on their arm, taking their hand, gushing."

"To Fred?"

"Oh, to any man. Even to Anthony."

Mary laughed. "Now that would be a pair."

"Maybe they are. Anthony is the only bachelor she has left."

"How was Roger's class?"

"Wonderful. He's always wonderful. Your father was a professor, wasn't he?"

Mary brightened at the reminder. "I only wish he had lived long enough to meet Roger Knight. And Phil, of course. He would have liked them as much as my mother and I do. Of course my father was very different from Roger, subdued, formal in a nice way. He was a poet, you know."

"Published?"

"Yes. One book."

"Oh, I must read it. Is it in the library?"

"I'll give you a copy." She leaned toward Griselda. "And I'll tell you a secret. We have two unopened boxes of the book in the attic."

7 Father Carmody was an old man who had seen much. The Notre Dame to which he had come as a boy had grown beyond the dreams or plans of anyone at the time, but Carmody had found it all organic and had played a significant part in the stages that had brought the university to its present eminence. He had played a role in the replacement of Terry Brennan in the fifties, he had been a power behind the scenes throughout the golden Hesburgh years. Change is welcome in youth and even in middle age but when hair turns gray and slowly disappears, it is more difficult to equate change with improvement. Still, Father Carmody did not repine. Nor did he, as so many of the congregation did, resist transfer to Holy Cross House when he seemed to have entered the final act of his long life. The naming of Roger Knight to the Huneker Chair of Catholic Studies had been considered his parting shot. The donor was an old friend, the appointment was more or less in his gift, pace the restrictions of an altered policy on recruitment and hiring, and he had formed a close friendship with Roger and his brother Phil.

"Don't get too curious about Huneker," he advised Roger.

"Oh, but I've already looked him up."

"Then you must be surprised that his name should be attached to a chair at Notre Dame."

"No more surprised than that I should be asked to fill it. Of course I have the wherewithal to fill a chair in the physical sense," Roger said as he patted the enormous orb of his belly.

The death of Fred Neville had pained Father Carmody. He had known the man only slightly, meeting him at the Knights' apartment, but had quickly included him in the affection he felt for Roger and his brother. Roger's monograph on the soi-disant Baron Corvo had captured Father Carmody's eye and quickly replaced Symon's *The Quest For Corvo* as his favorite book on that equivocal person. He had particularly liked Roger's handling of the break between Corvo and Robert Hugh Benson.

"Benson lectured here, you know."

Roger said, "I am prepared to believe that anyone interesting must have lectured here."

"Dick Sullivan was a great devotee of the writing of Corvo. Do you know the name?"

"Tell me."

Sullivan was one of the luminaries of the English department when all the luminaries bore only master's degrees. He had written a book about Notre Dame, as well as some quite successful popular fiction. In his last years, bearded, unobtrusive, he had moved about the campus all but unnoticed by brasher new arrivals. "He put me on to *The Desire and Pursuit of the Whole*."

"I'm surprised there isn't a Corvo chair, Father."

"Oh, we'll never be as daring as that."

A long life and a wide perspective had enabled Father Carmody to be philosophical about difficulties that seemed unprecedented. His motto might have been, This too will pass. But with the indictment of Tom McTear, the university was becoming the object of unwelcome curiosity on the part of the media.

"I am reliably told that a young fellow at the Joyce Center is planning to write a book about the case. Of course you know the kind of book he has in mind."

"No *In Quest Of Neville*?"

"Good Lord, no. Symons wrote a masterpiece. Since excelled, needless to say. This would be what is accurately called a non-book."

"Who is the young fellow?"

"Anthony Boule."

Father Carmody had succeeded in surprising Roger. But he had more in mind in mentioning it to him. "I wonder if you could have a word with him."

No need to say more. Discretion is the better part of such advice. The old priest went on to review the case against McTear, with an eye to imagining what Anthony might make of it if he went ahead with his plans, until Phil joined them to review the details of the investigation.

The fact that Tom McTear had been in Chicago when Fred Neville's body was found, and for some days before, was no alibi, given the way in which the murder had been accomplished. His motive was described in the newspapers as opposition to the connection between Fred and Naomi.

"The real reason is deeper. A visceral hatred of Notre Dame."

"Ah."

"And the church. But Notre Dame provided focus, and Fred a more narrow focus still."

"I have met the type," Father Carmody said sadly.

Phil went on. Apart from motive, there was opportunity. Despite his loathing for

Notre Dame, Tom McTear apparently could not stay away. When in town he often was given the use of one of the bedrooms in an apartment owned by his sister's cable channel. He was in it on the weekend before Fred dropped out of circulation. The discovery of the container of poison in the trash taken from that apartment might point to the sister as well as the brother. But her subsequent death seemed to rule her out. The fact that she had access to Fred's apartment, letting herself in after his death and brewing herself a fatal Irish coffee, was proof of that. The ingenious McTear was supposed to have learned of his sister's key and made use of it.

"Then she wouldn't have had it."

"Not necessarily. He could have returned it. He may have had it copied."

"Any proof of that?"

"No." Phil said it reluctantly. Nothing exposes the strengths and weaknesses of a case against someone more than such a narration of it.

"Don't forget Santander," Roger said. He had been silent during his brother's tale. "He identified Naomi as having been there at the apartment the day before Fred's body was found."

"Roger, the fact that she brewed herself a fatal cup of coffee indicates that she did not know the cannister was doctored."

Roger was roused by his brother's hastening over difficulties in the prosecutor's case against Tom McTear, and developed an account of his own.

"Say it was indeed Naomi who arranged things so that Fred would eventually administer the coup de grâce to himself. I talked with her hours before she drank that lethal cup of coffee. She was a divided woman, telling me things it is difficult to imagine her volunteering to the stranger I was. But what if she had decided to do what she did, the ultimate recompense for killing the man she claimed to love. She left here, drove to the apartment, let herself in and romantically recalled other visits to the apartment. Then, resolved, she brewed the coffee and put herself beyond the reach of the law."

Phil stared at his brother and was obviously disturbed by the ease with which he had constructed this scenario.

"Do think that is what happened, Roger?"

"About as much as I believe your account."

"My account? I am telling you what the

259

prosecutor thinks. And, I might add, Jimmy Stewart."

"You spoke as if you thought it true."

"I do!"

But there was bravura rather than confidence in Phil's voice. The conversation turned to other things and soon Phil slipped away to the television. Father Carmody went back to the threatening non-book about Notre Dame's murder scandal.

"How did you hear of it, Father?"

"From a young man I counseled for a time. He was thinking of entering the congregation but came to see he had no vocation."

"Would you be breaking a confidence by telling me his name?"

"Certainly not. He is in a rage. A rage I cannot sympathize with. The idea for the book was originally his. His name is Scott Frye."

8 Roger Knight was able to get around campus with ease in a golf cart, but for ventures beyond he was dependent on his brother Phil and others. While Phil had a moderate-sized vehicle for his own use it had been necessary to refit a van to accommodate Roger. The central area was dominated by a swivel seat that could describe, in stages, a 360° turn, and no matter which direction Roger faced he was able to have his computer before him. In this van the Knight brothers made their journeys, avoiding air travel as much as possible, since there was no way in which Roger could fit into a single seat. Of late, given the various campaigns against obesity, hostility was added to discomfort, and they eschewed the airways entirely. Of course when Phil traveled alone he traveled in the ordinary manner.

The charge that Father Carmody had placed on Roger made travel off campus necessary, although initially, in his trip to the Joyce Center, his golf cart had sufficed. Since Griselda was with him, he turned the wheel over to her.

"I want to talk to Anthony Boule," Roger

said in reply to Griselda's question.

"Look, any inquiry about sports he can answer I can probably answer too."

"I want to learn who the point guard on the women's basketball team is this year."

Griselda slowed the cart and stared at him. "Are you serious?"

"No."

"Meaning you don't want me to know why we're going?"

"You will be with me all the time and will soon know as much as I do."

"Fat chance."

"Precisely."

"Oh, I didn't mean —"

"Always take credit for wit, whether intended or not."

Roger hoped that he would not have to talk to Anthony. The secretary, Thelma, would do. As he understood it, she had been among the group Tom McTear had invited to the network apartment to watch a game in comfort. Perhaps she could give him Scott's address so that he could arrange for a meeting without alarming Anthony. Scott put himself in the position of the aggrieved and his complaint was against Anthony who was unlikely to be a forthcoming font of information about his new-won foe.

Griselda rolled them right up to the door of the building and parked.

"I will be ticketed and towed."

She shook her head. "They'll figure it belongs to a banged-up jock."

"Are athletes beyond the law?"

"Only in season."

The glass double doors of the sports-information department slid aside at their approach and Roger waddled through, Griselda effectively concealed behind him. The girl at the receptionist desk looked up. Her eyes widened, her mouth opened, she raised a hand and lowered her glasses, she stared. Griselda came out from behind him.

"Thelma, this is Professor Knight."

She lifted dreamily to her feet and held out a hand. "Oh, we've met."

"So we have. I am as unlikely to have forgotten you."

Her chin tucked in in doubt. "Me?"

Griselda said, "Do you have a chair? A large chair?"

The search for an adequate chair occupied the next few minutes. Finally, it was decided that Roger would be least uncomfortable in the armless chair that Thelma used, a secretary's chair. Lowering himself tentatively into it, Roger judged that it would do, at least for the short time he was here. "I feel that I am perched on one of those things golf fans unfold."

"Have you really come to see me?" Thelma said, obviously delighted to be at the center of all this fuss.

"I need your help. I believe you know Scott Frye."

Thelma had sat upon her desk after surrendering her chair to Roger. Now she slid along it away from him. Her receptive manner gave way to a receptionist manner.

"Scott."

"He works at a place called the Hoosier Residences."

Thelma said nothing.

"Where Naomi McTear stayed. And her brother," Griselda said.

"But why have you come here?"

"Oh, it's probably only a baseless rumor. Scott came to my good friend Father Carmody saying that a book about the Tom McTear trial was being planned and I wanted to speak to him about it."

"It is baseless. Scott couldn't write his way out of a wet paper bag."

"You're sure of that?"

The door of Fred's office opened and Anthony came out, preoccupied, papers fluttering in his hand. He stopped abruptly at the sight of Roger Knight. He looked at Thelma.

"Why don't you help this gentleman, Anthony," Thelma said. And to Roger, "We can wheel the chair right into that office."

"Anything at all," Anthony said, but he was puzzled, perhaps by the expression on Thelma's face and her tone of voice. But the secretary came into the office too and so did Griselda. Anthony took the chair from behind the desk and rolled it free, perhaps not wanting to seem to usurp Fred's office. The time for obliquity and indirection was past.

Roger said, "Your friend Scott Frye told Father Carmody that you have stolen an idea he had for a book about the McTear trial."

"Stolen!" Thelma said. "How can you steal an idea?"

Roger nodded. "A good point. The sense in which our ideas are ours is unrelated to their content."

Silence fell.

"Of course there can be ownership of a sort. Plagiarism is a case in point."

Anthony was aroused. "It's true that Scott and I talked about such a book. He seemed to think I would write it and he would get credit. Such a thought could occur to anyone but if they are unable to write how can they have a claim on it?"

"And you have claimed it?"

"I am giving serious consideration to writing such a book."

"I can see the attraction of the idea," Roger said. "Publishers seem drawn to such books, don't they? Exposse, sensational treatments. I can also see why Father Carmody thinks the university would not be well-served by such a book."

Thelma came around to face Roger. "Anyone could have that idea. Maybe others already have. The university can't stop such a project."

Roger looked up at her. "Are you involved in it too?"

She stepped back. She looked at Anthony. Anthony said, "If I go ahead it will be a joint product."

"Ah."

"Coauthors."

Roger switched gears. He smiled at Thelma. "I really have to get a chair like this. It's quite comfortable." As if in proof he spun around. Griselda stopped him as if he were the great globe itself. He ended facing Anthony. "You must have given a lot of thought to recent events. Fred's death,

Naomi's, the arrest of Tom McTear."

"That will be the meat of the book."

"Do you think Tom is guilty?"

"The book will follow the trial process. The jury will determine who did it. Or who they think did it. I suppose it could have been any number of people other than Tom McTear."

"He did it," Thelma said flatly.

Roger swung back to her. "It certainly looks that way, doesn't it? I would hate to be his defense lawyer."

"But what is punishment nowadays?" Anthony said.

Roger said, "For me, the mystery is how Tom McTear could have gotten into the apartment to poison the coffee in the cannister."

"Maybe Fred let him in?"

Roger shook his head. "And left him alone to poison his coffee? If it was just his cup that had been poisoned, conceivably that could have been done surreptitiously. But the whole cannister?" Roger looked around as if in bewilderment. "Of course that begs the question of his getting in. He must have done it when Fred wasn't there. In that way he could be far off when Fred made use of the poisoned coffee."

Anthony nodded. "That is a problem."

"Santander could have let him in," Thelma said.

Anthony shook his head. "He would have mentioned that by now if he had."

"It seems a small point," Thelma said.

"He couldn't have gotten at your keys," Anthony said with a laugh.

"No way. He's never been in the office so far as I know."

"Your keys?"

"People leave keys to their homes and cars and apartments here with Thelma. In case of loss, so their mail can be taken in when they're away, whatever."

Roger nodded. "One theory is that he took the key from Naomi's purse. After all, she must have had a key."

Thelma grew animated. "How else could she have gotten into the apartment the other day?"

"That must be it."

They ended on a happy note of agreement. Anthony accompanied them out to the golf cart, Thelma having repossessed her chair.

"It may fall through, you know. The book. It's still just an idea an agent is trying to peddle. Tell Father Carmody that."

"And to pray that the deal doesn't go through?"

Anthony looked back at the closed double glass doors.

"As far as I'm concerned, I hope it doesn't. I don't want to do anything to jeopardize my position here."

As they drove away, Griselda said, "His position? He's one rung above Thelma."

"And what rung is hers?"

"The one below his."

Roger said, "What got Mary Shuster off was the mug book of people in the administration, all rungs and ranks. There is one for the faculty too, and another for the chaired professors."

"And one for the athletic department."

"Do you have one?"

"I could get one."

"Now?"

Griselda made a U-turn and headed back to the Joyce Center. Roger waited in the cart, his hood pulled over his head, while she went inside again. She hurried past the double doors of sports information and went out of sight. Five minutes later she was back.

"Got it. I assume you want to see my picture."

"I hated to ask directly."

She punched his arm. "Home?"

"Where is your car?"

"You want to go someplace else?"

"If you'll take me."

9   Young Jacuzzi in the prosecutor's office was understandably affected by the attention the case against Tom McTear had attracted. The media were in from everywhere, some perhaps anxious to see a colleague fall, others more sympathetic, all intent on squeezing every last line, byte or footage from the events at the St. Joseph County Courthouse, Judge Jerry Frese presiding. Jacuzzi had made himself available to the press with a prodigality that had brought a rebuke from the judge.

"I know it's old-fashioned, Graham, but I think courtrooms are where cases should be tried, not out on the steps. With all this snow and ice you might fall and break an arm."

Laughter in the court. Maybe if judges learned how to express themselves otherwise than in multiply qualified sentences they would be interviewed more often themselves. Jacuzzi, a young man, did not question the desirability of exposure to the media. The fleeting fame associated with this seems timeless while it endures and second thoughts come afterward, if at all.

Jacuzzi was not loath to suggest to the press that the case against McTear was a lock. Not even the laconic briefings of Jimmy Stewart raised doubt in his youthful mind.

"Of course it's all circumstantial," Stewart said, stopping Jacuzzi in full flight.

"You mean we don't have video footage of him putting the poison in the coffee cannister?"

"Where did he get the poison? Did he buy it, did he steal it?"

"Aren't the Chicago police looking into that?"

"In between more pressing duties. Don't count on a bill of sale turning up. And of course there are no fingerprints of McTear anywhere in Fred Neville's apartment."

"Gloves."

Stewart did not tell him that no prints of McTear had been found in the Hoosier Residence apartment where undoubtedly he had stayed. The cleanup crew there really cleaned up.

"Nor did anyone ever see him enter Fred's apartment, let alone when Fred was missing from his office."

Of course Jacuzzi had responses to all these. But his strategy was to fix in the jury's mind that McTear had motive and opportunity and blur such difficulties as Stewart was raising.

"You think he's innocent?"

Stewart said, "Guilty as sin."

"So why are you giving me such a hard time?"

"I'm a Cubs fan."

"You wouldn't want a murderer doing play-by-play."

Stewart let it go. "But your main problem will be how he got into the building in the first place."

"With a key."

"Where did he get it?"

"From Naomi."

"Too bad she isn't here to back that up. Besides it begs a question. Did she herself have a key?"

"Oh come on. She let herself in."

Teresa, the supposed cousin of Santander? Stewart let it go. A nagging thought returned, one expressed by Phil Knight. They had not questioned the girl who had been with Santander on one occasion, a girl who worked in the building. She must have a master key. Had she let anyone into Fred's apartment at the relevant times? Investigators for the defense would surely think of that. Well, not surely. Maybe. Stewart called Phil and asked if he was up to a little detective work.

"As little as possible."

"This won't take long."

"The game starts at eight."

IO "If it's got to be one of you, I'll take you," Santander said, when Roger had succeeded in rousing the manager.

"I won't tell my brother."

"Which one is your brother?"

"The one who has the same parents I do."

Santander accepted that. "So what is it this time?"

"I hate to talk in the hall."

"I was just going to ask you in." Santander had been casting incontinent eyes at Griselda during this exchange with Roger. "Don't I know you?"

"I don't know."

"You look familiar."

"She is a star athlete," Roger said. "She plays basketball for Notre Dame."

"That must be it."

"Do you ever watch?"

"I must have seen you in the paper."

"Her photograph?" Roger said. He had made it to the couch and now lowered himself on to the middle cushion of three. "Precisely why I am here." He took the mug book Griselda had given him and thumbed through it. He found what he was looking for. "There. That is Griselda."

Santander compared the page with Griselda who was shedding her jacket in the overheated apartment. "Sure," he said.

Roger was turning the pages. He stopped and pointed. Santander stared and then looked at Roger.

"Familiar?"

Santander nodded slowly. "I should have remembered."

"Who is it?" Griselda asked.

She might have been anticipating the knock on the door. Santander had not restored the security chain after admitting Roger and Griselda and there was nothing to impede Thelma's entry.

"Well, well," Thelma said, locking the door but not putting the chain in place.

Roger looked at Thelma sadly. "So you realized how stupid it was to mention Santander and those keys?"

"And that you're not stupid enough not to pick up on it. I'm sorry about this." She did not sound sorry.

"Are you going to make coffee for us?"

Thelma smiled. "Pretty good, eh? If Naomi hadn't paid one last sentimental visit to Fred's apartment no one would have known. I blame myself. I should have gotten rid of that cannister."

"In the trash at Hoosier Residences?"

Thelma laughed bitterly. "No matter how much you plan, something is bound to go wrong."

Santander had been following this with growing alarm and began inching toward the back of his apartment. Still facing Thelma and Roger and Griselda, he got the bedroom doorknob in his hands and slowly turned it. But before he could open it and slip into his bedroom Teresa pulled the door open from the inside and Santander tumbled backward into the room. This distracted Thelma. Griselda in one graceful movement rose and brought the side of her hand down on the secretary's neck. Thelma slumped to the floor. In the confusion, Teresa made a hasty exit.

"Good work," Roger said to Griselda. "It might be wise to tie her up."

PART FIVE

TENDER IS
THE KNIGHT

I   A pounding on the door announced the arrival of Phil and Stewart. Since Griselda was busy tying Thelma's wrists and ankles, Roger rose from the couch and lumbered to the door. When he opened it, two surprised faces stared at him. Well, three. Jimmy had a firm grip on the arm of a squirming Teresa who was sputtering in Spanish.

"Roger!"

But Phil's eyes fell to where the bound Thelma was coming groggily back to the real world. Jimmy ushered Teresa inside and Phil followed.

"There's your murderer," Roger said.

Santander appeared in the bedroom door and looked wildly about. The presence of Teresa did not soothe him.

"That's a lie!" he cried, but he was ignored. A guilty man feels universally vulnerable, but Santander's misdeeds did not include murder. Teresa directed her flow of Spanish at Santander.

"What the hell is she saying?" Stewart asked.

"You wouldn't want to know," Roger said. "Thelma, perhaps you would like to

281

tell Lieutenant Stewart what you've been up to."

But the safeguards of contemporary criminal investigation were invoked by Stewart.

"You tell me, Roger."

Roger returned to the couch where in comfort he told Thelma's story, not without repeated tries of intervention from Thelma, immediately shushed by Stewart. Griselda had helped Thelma to her feet with the brusqueness she might have aided a bowled-over opponent on the basketball court and plunked her into a chair. In a blow for modesty, she covered the bared legs of the bound receptionist with a Notre Dame blanket that had been rolled up and placed on the back of the couch.

If Stewart was surprised to learn that Thelma was the murderer he had sought, and thought he had found in Tom McTear, he gave little sign of it.

It was Phil who wondered what Thelma's motive could possibly be.

"Love," Roger said simply.

"Love!" Thelma cried.

"Love thwarted. Love twisted. Love spurned."

"I don't get it," Phil said.

"Don't explain me!" Thelma shrieked. "You couldn't begin to understand."

Understanding, however partial, came in the following days. Jimmy took Thelma away and Phil went with him, handing her into the back seat of Stewart's car. Downtown, the prosecutor was informed of the new turn of events, Tom McTear was released with Maurice Gibbons muttering about a suit for false arrest, harassment, and other indictable offenses, but these were merely pro forma. The lawyer preferred creating the impression that it was his legal skill that had brought about the liberation of his client. Thelma secured the services of Emil Zollar, a local attorney, but nothing could stop her now from talking. Zollar tried in vain to shut her up but she was determined to cast herself in the role of avenging angel. The phrase was Roger's.

"Angel?" Phil asked.

"There are fallen angels, Phil."

Thelma produced the microcassette from Fred's telephone from her purse. Why had she taken it?

"Listen to it and you will see."

It made melancholy listening. In recorded message after recorded message,

Thelma had sought in vain to interest Fred in herself. This recorded persona had contrasted with her relatively subdued manner at work, where she had contented herself with batting her lashes at Fred, but then she batted her lashes at every man.

It was Fred's susceptibility to both Naomi McTear and Mary Shuster that had encouraged rather than discouraged the enamored Thelma. If two, why not three? She had come to believe that Fred's affection was indiscriminate but that, once he was smitten by her, he would swiftly become monogamous.

"It's almost too easy," Stewart complained on a visit to the Knight brothers.

Thelma had an uncle who ran a nursery and it was there that she had obtained the strychnine. Of course she had a key to Fred's apartment, so there was no problem of access to his kitchen and coffee canister when her passion turned from desire to hatred. She had been in the group that had benefitted from Tom McTear's play-by-play in the apartment at Hoosier Residences and thus had opportunity to drop the container stolen from her uncle's nursery into the trash. Had she intended to incriminate Tom McTear?

"More likely Naomi," Roger mused.

"Right. And that might have worked. Naomi was a more promising suspect than her brother."

When Naomi had made coffee in Fred's apartment and drank what might have been intended as a farewell cup to her departed beloved, suspicion had transferred to Tom McTear.

"He could have been found guilty," Stewart said.

Silence followed this reminder of the contingencies of crime and punishment and the tantalizing non-convergence of legal and moral guilt.

2 Notre Dame's male basketball team faltered as the season progressed but the Lady Irish were on their way to another national title. Griselda was a major cause of this success and on the floor she gave her mind totally to the game. But her ambition to lead a life like Roger Knight's grew ever stronger. However, she was beginning to find it hard to share her mentor's esteem for the novels of Maurice Francis Egan.

"Not all writers are major writers, Griselda."

"He wouldn't even sit on the bench."

"De gustibus non disputandum est." Roger crossed his fingers as he said this. The phrase suggested that literary judgments are mere expressions of subjective feeling, which was heresy to him.

"I'm going to take Latin," Griselda said.

"It's about time."

And so the conversation turned to latinity, the Tridentine rite, the woeful liturgical translations, the great evolution from classical through medieval and Renaissance Latin. And inevitably the poem Fred had written for Mary Shuster came up.

286

Mary's reaction to the arrest of Thelma Maynooth was something of a surprise.

"It's awful to say, but I had half-hoped it was Naomi. If she could do that it would prove she didn't really love Fred."

" 'Each man kills the thing he loves,' " Roger murmured.

"Who says so?"

Her answer was the recitation of a large swatch of *The Ballad of Reading Gaol*. Mrs. Shuster was enthralled.

"Nathaniel loved that poem. He was a little sheepish about it but he too had it by heart."

"A priest visited Wilde on his deathbed in Paris," Roger said. "Although there is a dispute as to what priest it was."

"Who was Isadore of Seville?" Mary asked.

But Phil intervened before Roger could get going.

"You should get credits for living with him," Griselda said.

"And grow dumber by degrees?"

But it was time for popcorn and Roger donned his apron and went to work in the kitchen. Griselda rose to help him.

"Did you hear about Anthony Boule?" she asked.

"What?"

"He's out of a job."

"Fired?"

"His position has been eliminated."

"But not Fred's, certainly."

"There'll be a national search. Anthony can apply for it, I suppose. I wouldn't give much for his chances."

"But he dropped the idea of the book."

"What book?"

But of course the proposed book had gone the way of most such ideas for instant fame and fortune. It would have had to become the story of Thelma, and Anthony had no interest in that. He had been reconciled with Scott Frye and would himself be working in the Hoosier Residence until he knew the outcome of his application to succeed Fred.

"Scott is talking about a screenplay," Anthony said, avoiding Roger's eyes.

"Will you collaborate?"

"Ha! I'm cured of the writing bug."

3 A month before Thelma Maynooth's trial a bearded figure showed up at Roger's campus office.

"Professor Knight? My name is Greg Maieutic."

Professor Maieutic, as it turned out, taught creative writing at IUSB.

"I'm having a crisis of conscience," Maieutic said, taking the chair Roger had indicated.

Roger, uneasy, said nothing.

"I had Thelma Maynooth in class. A night class."

"A writing class?"

Maieutic nodded. "I speak to you in confidence. She wrote a novel for the course. Just began it during the semester, but she would come to see me from time to time and by gosh she finished it." He ran his fingers through his beard. "I suppose I don't have to tell you how rare that is. People think they want to write . . ." His voice trailed away, taking with it a thousand faded hopes of authorial success. He looked at Roger. "The novel might have been a scenario for what has happened. Of course it was autobiographical."

"I'd like to see it."

"Would you? I was hoping you would. That's why I came. You'd have to read the novel to understand my problem."

Meanwhile Laura Reith and Tom McTear were seeing a lot of one another. Phil had gotten the news from Stewart.

"Hasn't he already had his quota of wives?"

"He's going to have them annulled."

Roger wondered if a church wedding would soften McTear's attitude toward Notre Dame.

"Jimmy says Laura wants to get married in Sacred Heart."

Roger did come into possession of *Drink To Me Only*, a mystery novel by Thelma Maynooth. Roger read it through in one sitting that night, fascinated, though not by any literary merits it had. Thelma's command of English was shaky, but then she was mimicking who-knew-what models in the mystery genre. Maieutic had called it autobiographical and that was certainly true. Despite the stilted prose, Roger recognized the office in which Thelma had worked. The heroine was a vulnerable young woman who succumbed to the advances of a married man. As Roger read, western music was playing on Phil's radio and a lyric captured the theme of the novel. A good-hearted woman in love with a two-timing man. But her good heart had been sorely tested when the heroine learned that her lover had a wife. The scene in which the two women met was one of the best in the book, and it provided the motivation for what happened. Rita, the heroine, decided to do herself and the wife a favor and send Howard the husband into the arms of St. Peter. Her weapon was Irish coffee.

Two days later Roger met with Maieutic again.

"Have you read it?"

"Yes."

"Pretty bad?"

"But fascinating."

"You can see my problem. Should I show it to the police? It would go against all my principles, academic principles, but I am a citizen as well as a professor."

"I don't think there is any need to show it to the police," Roger said. "They have a strong case without it. She has all but confessed, but even so the evidence is overwhelming."

Maieutic let out a great sigh. "I can't tell you how relieved that makes me."

"I suppose you could return it to Thelma."

"I will. I will. That novel has been an albatross around my neck."

And he did return *Drink To Me Only* to Thelma and, after her conviction, she contacted an agent who showed interest given Thelma's current address. She telephoned Roger to gloat. And in a way to express her gratitude.

"You may have found me out," she said. "But you made me a writer."

Not even God could do that, Roger thought. Of course he congratulated her and then spent half an hour pondering the depths to which publishing had fallen.

"At least she didn't call it *Irish Coffee*," Greg Whelan said wryly.

"God forbid."

About the Author

Ralph McInerny is the author of more than thirty books, including the popular Father Dowling mystery series, and has taught for more than forty years at the University of Notre Dame, where he is the director of the Jacques Maritain Center. He has been awarded the Bouchercon Lifetime Achievement Award and was recently appointed to the President's Committee on the Arts and Humanities. He lives in South Bend, Indiana.

The employees of Thorndike Press hope you have enjoyed this Large Print book. All our Thorndike and Wheeler Large Print titles are designed for easy reading, and all our books are made to last. Other Thorndike Press Large Print books are available at your library, through selected bookstores, or directly from us.

For information about titles, please call:

(800) 223-1244

or visit our Web site at:

www.gale.com/thorndike
www.gale.com/wheeler

To share your comments, please write:

Publisher
Thorndike Press
295 Kennedy Memorial Drive
Waterville, ME   04901